Gray Shadows

Julia Gousseva

ISBN-13: 978-1500804992
ISBN-10: 1500804991

Gray Shadows

Chapter One

Nikolai slipped his Makarov pistol into the shoulder holster, put on his jacket, and stepped outside. He checked the time: a quarter to ten. As agreed, his client's black Audi was parked on the corner. Everything was exactly like it was supposed to be. So far, the only unusual thing that winter morning was the bright sun that enveloped Moscow with a surreal warm glow.

He squinted and crossed the street, looking for things out of place, for anything different, anything that suggested a possibility of danger. He passed by a small playground where two young mothers were pushing their toddlers on the swings. An elderly couple, hand in hand, walked by him. A middle-aged man turned the corner and kept going, his black poodle on a long leash. So far, nothing looked alarming.

At twenty-eight years old, tall, fit, muscular, and with prior military experience, Nikolai was one of the most sought-after bodyguards in the prestigious Centurion Personal Protection Agency in Moscow. Nikolai credited his success to his attention to detail and his ability to maintain his cool even in the most extreme circumstances, and his job provided plenty of such circumstances.

Nikolai's younger and less experienced colleagues joked that he was as meticulous and as thorough as someone suffering from paranoia. Nikolai took such comments as a compliment because his so-called paranoia had saved more than one client's life, and Nikolai's own life, on more than a few occasions.

As he neared the familiar four-story building, Nikolai closed his left eye in preparation for the darkness inside, a trick that cut the eyesight adjustment time in half. He opened the heavy spring-loaded door, stepped inside and started walking up the steps to the top floor, looking for anything that could be a threat. Business as usual.

His goal was to detect any changes from the day before, check for anything potentially lethal, and eliminate it. On the landing between the second and third floor, a piece of cardboard was stuck behind a radiator. That was a change, so Nikolai carefully pulled it out, inspected it, and swept the ray of his flashlight all around the radiator: nothing. On the third floor, an old kitchen sink was leaning against the wall. Another change. Probably, someone was remodeling, but Nikolai had to be sure. He lifted the sink, scaring a white cat that meowed angrily and ran up the steps. Nothing behind the sink. So far so good.

Nikolai kept walking up, all the way to the top. He inspected the floor by the door to the attic: it was clean and shiny, which meant that nobody had been inside the attic. The day before, Nikolai had sprinkled a thin line of powdered chalk right by the door. The line was barely visible, but if somebody had opened the door and walked around, Nikolai's flashlight would have revealed white chalky traces. There was nothing.

Nikolai took one last look around, ran down to the second floor, and rang the doorbell. Vasily Petrovich, his client of the last three months, opened the door and motioned for Nikolai to come in. Vasily Petrovich was a tall, broad-shouldered man in his late thirties, but looked closer to mid-forties. His face was youthful, but his manner and formal suits suggested someone more mature, a man who grew up too fast, like many of his generation and social status.

Nikolai liked and respected Vasily Petrovich: he was smart, rational, and level-headed. He was also an honest and genuinely good person, and that made working for him so much easier. Money was not enough for Nikolai to continually put his life at risk; he had to have respect for his client and believe that saving that client's life was a worthy endeavor. Nikolai often wondered how Vasily Petrovich managed to work as a lawyer for the government and resist corruption. His honesty was part of the reason for Nikolai's presence.

Vasily Petrovich called the Centurion Agency after a wave of high-profile murders of judges, prosecutors, and prominent businessmen swept through Moscow. Even though no direct threats were made against Vasily Petrovich, contentious disagreements were frequent and unpredictable at the current period of transition from government-owned to privately owned property. And many such disagreements got settled in the streets, with guns and car bombs. Vasily Petrovich needed a bodyguard to help him avoid falling victim to one such disagreement.

Today, Nikolai was to accompany Vasily Petrovich to a meeting between the Russian government and potential investors.

Vasily Petrovich buttoned his coat and picked up his briefcase.

"Ready to go?" Nikolai said.

"Ready if you are."

The tension in Vasily Petrovich's voice was palpable. Nikolai had witnessed enough of such meetings to know how heated and unpredictable they could get. The constantly changing investment, tax, and business laws made coming to practical agreements difficult, and the prospect of enormous monetary gains or losses trumped existing laws, pushing the participants to find other ways to settle disputes after the meeting, often outside of the legal realm. Nikolai's job started right where the civilized disputes ended.

Vasily Petrovich lit a cigarette, and they walked downstairs. As usual, they did not talk much. Nikolai needed to stay focused on the surrounding circumstances.

He also did not want to get too emotionally close to Vasily Petrovich. Getting too friendly with clients could lead to loss of vigilance, potentially fatal for both. Danger was especially likely when it was least expected.

When they reached the first floor, Nikolai opened the front door and stepped outside first, his Makarov at the ready. He looked up and down the street.

Nothing. He motioned for Vasily Petrovich to come out.

As soon as the two of them were out on the street, an old truck, its bed covered with thick black tarp, careened around the corner and hit the brakes, coming to a screeching halt.

"Get back inside!" Nikolai shouted even before he saw the long gun barrel appear from under the tarp. Multiple shots were fired, and Nikolai shot back, aiming alternately at the tarp and at the wheels. He pushed Vasily Petrovich down on the ground, back towards the building entrance. Immediately, Nikolai felt a sharp searing pain in his left leg and saw blood on Vasily Petrovich's coat.

Ignoring the pain, Nikolai kept shooting as he struggled to get them both back inside the building.

The thud of the heavy door slamming shut shielded them from the thundering gunfire. And almost at the same time, Nikolai heard the whine of a revved-up truck engine, followed by the screeching of tires. Nikolai reached for his phone to call the ambulance. All sounds faded and everything went dark.

The next sound Nikolai heard were voices he couldn't recognize, low mechanical humming, and faint footsteps. He listened for a little longer before opening his eyes, trying to get oriented. When he opened his eyes, he saw exactly what he had expected: he was in a hospital bed, with medical machines, monitors, and tubes connected to him.

"Nikolai! You're awake!" he heard Olga's voice from the corner. A second later, she was next to him, taking his hand in hers.

Olga sat down on the chair next to his bed. She smiled. It was a bittersweet smile, with relief, love and worry mixed together. Her dark hair was pulled back in a ponytail. She looked a little tired and even thinner than usual. She tended to lose weight when she was stressed, and that was a lot lately, largely because of Nikolai's job.

"I was so worried about you!" Olga said. "How are you feeling?"

"Alive," Nikolai said.

"Do you need anything?" Olga said. "Besides all that." She pointed to the bedside table.

He turned his head to the side and saw a large basket of fruit and a teddy bear.

"I feel like a real sick person with all these gifts."

"The fruit is from Vasily Petrovich. It's been here since yesterday morning. And the teddy bear is from me."

"Thank you, Olechka. Did you say yesterday morning? How long have I been here?"

"Forty-eight hours, most of them unconscious."

"That's a long time. How's Vasily Petrovich?"

"Just fine. He was treated and released. Nothing serious, thanks to you. Just a few scrapes and bruises, mostly from the fall. No bullet wounds. He was worried about you and said you were a real hero." Olga's voice cracked a little, and she looked away for a moment.

"And he's got real enemies," Nikolai said.

"Do you know who was after him?" Olga said. "And after you?"

Nikolai wished he could tell Olga that the assailants had been caught and were about to be prosecuted and put in prison for a long time. But that would be a blatant lie, a lie that Olga would not believe.

"Not exactly, but I have my suspicions," Nikolai said, settling for a half-lie.

He had no idea who the guys in the truck were, and even if they were ever found, the odds of which were lower than winning the Moscow City Lottery, they would never admit as to who had hired them. Most likely, they did not know who it was as the order would have been handed down through a string of intermediaries, none of whom knew the whole chain of command. The only thing Nikolai was sure of is that this was no botched burglary. These guys were contract killers. Luckily for Nikolai and Vasily Petrovich, they were not the highest professionals.

Nikolai forced a smile. "Let's talk about something else. How are you doing? How's work?"

"Work is fine. Going to St. Petersburg for a few days to get some things finalized before the big presentation next week," Olga said.

"I'll take some time off and come with you."

Olga leaned in and kissed Nikolai gently. "That's a nice thought, but the doctor thinks you'll need to stay here for about five more days."

"I don't have to listen to the doctor. I can recover better in St. Petersburg."

"No, you can't. You have a lot of bone and soft tissue injuries, and they need to do some more X-rays on your knee now that the swelling has gone down."

"My knee will be just fine."

"I hope so. But to make sure that it is, you need to recover here, and not in St. Petersburg. But I'd love it if you came with me to the big corporate dinner party next week. That's where I will really need your support."

"I wouldn't miss it," Nikolai said.

"Great. But for now just rest, and I'll send the nurse to check on you. I'll call you in the morning, when I get to St. Petersburg." She smiled and waved from the door. "Take care of yourself. I'll be back soon!"

As soon as the door closed behind her, Nikolai stretched and rubbed his sore back. Lying in a hospital bed for two days did not do any favors for his physical condition or his morale. He did not like Olga to see him in this weak state; right now, he was not a good match to her energy and independence. He wanted to be strong for her. Always.

When he first met Olga, he was still a student at the Moscow Military Academy, planning for a career in the military, with a stable income, good benefits, and an ability to provide for his family. Most likely, that was what Olga expected at that time, too. All girls from the Pedagogical Institute who came to their Saturday night dances wanted a husband and children. Olga's teaching degree would have been a perfect match for his military career: teachers were needed in all cities, towns, and villages, so she would be guaranteed a job. That was then. Now, just a few years later, life was different.

Olga was amazing. Many of her college friends were barely surviving on their teacher salaries or were still looking for jobs, having a hard time finding their place in the new Russia. Olga adjusted to the new circumstances with ease, grace, and even a certain playfulness.

Nikolai realized that most men would have been ecstatic to have a woman like Olga in their lives and would have no qualms about accepting her love and attention, and reciprocating it. For a while, that was how Nikolai felt, too, but lately things have been changing.

Nikolai admired the way Olga had adjusted to the new life, but he liked the old Olga more. She used to be passionate about teaching, about making kids' lives better, and she was an idealist. When Nikolai used to think of their life together, he imagined her going to work at a school every morning, coming home in the afternoon, marking papers in the evenings, and sharing school stories with him, just like his mom did with his dad.

But that's not what happened. Olga's life now was all about business trips to St. Petersburg, fancy dinners, presentations, high heels, and business suits. It took her no time to apply her math degree to accounting. And she was quite successful, as evidenced by yet another likely promotion after this latest presentation. Nikolai felt out of place in her new world. Of course, his life was very different now, too, but he felt that at his core, he was still the same: the warrior, the protector, and the idealist.

His thoughts were interrupted by the opening door.

"Sleeping on the job?" Anatoly, his boss and the owner of the Centurion Personal Protection Agency, strolled into the room. As always, he looked elegant and dignified, his broad shoulders and muscular build accentuated by a well-tailored coat. In his mid-forties, he was still in a great shape, physically and mentally. He prided himself on not only running the administrative part of his agency but also teaching martial arts classes and getting personally involved with all the cases and clients. His life was busy, but he often told Nikolai that he could not imagine it any other way.

Anatoly looked around and smiled broadly. "Quite a resort here. And I'm paying for all this?"

"Nice to see you, too," Nikolai said. "What are you doing here? Things are slow at the office?"

"Things are always slow without you," Anatoly responded, pulled up a chair and sat down next to the bed.

"Which is not always bad." He chuckled, then his expression got serious. "You've had all of us worried. I'm glad you're looking and feeling better. "

"Thanks. Any news on the guys who tried to kill us?"

"Not much." Anatoly shook his head. "The police are investigating, but we both know what that means."

Nikolai nodded. "They're going to say it was a robbery, but nothing was taken. As usual."

"As they have said in similar cases, the robbery was botched because a passer-by scared them off."

"Right," Nikolai said. "So what do you think? Hired killers?"

"No doubt. The question is who hired them and why. Of course, we've always known that Vasily Petrovich has plenty of enemies."

"Has he told you any more about the meeting he was scheduled to attend the morning we got attacked?"

"Not yet. Why?" Anatoly said.

"He seemed stressed and tense about it, more than usual. We need to find out the details about it."

"I'll look into that, thanks. But you rest. We need you back healthy."

The next few days dragged on and on. The doctor insisted on keeping Nikolai in the hospital for more tests, observations, and physical therapy. Any objections on Nikolai's part were met with the doctor's stern comments, "Your boss told me that you will not observe the rest regimen at home if we discharge you early. So, we won't."

Finally, a week later, the doctor announced that Nikolai could be discharged. His leg was mostly healed, and the soreness in his back was going away. Nikolai was ready to get back to work, but when he mentioned the idea to the doctor, the doctor shook his head and said, "Your job for the next few weeks is to use a cane and get plenty of rest. Nothing else."

Nikolai was fine with using the cane. But plenty of rest? That was questionable.

He could never deal well with rest or too much idle time. Plus, he was all alone since Olga was still in St. Petersburg, so rest meant boredom and loneliness.

As soon as his hospital release papers were signed, Nikolai took a taxi to Anatoly's office, a small two-story building with a tall wrought-iron fence around it. Nikolai pushed the intercom button, looked up, and waved to the camera mounted on top of the gate. The lock buzzed, Nikolai pulled on the gate, and walked inside.

The security guard greeted Nikolai, and Nikolai headed to Anatoly's office located at the north end of the long hallway. The walls were painted light brown and decorated with prints of Moscow cityscapes.

The door to Anatoly's office was open. Anatoly sat at his desk, busy with a thick file and two laptops at the same time.

"May I?" Nikolai said.

Anatoly looked up as soon as Nikolai walked in, leaning on the cane.

"You're looking sophisticated," Anatoly said. "With that cane, you could pass for a writer or an artist. What brings you here? Shouldn't you be at home resting?"

Nikolai shrugged. "I can't handle playing patient anymore. I need an assignment. Anything."

"You are not ready to work with clients yet. Not with that cane and a limp. Also, the doctor said two more weeks of rest." Anatoly shook his head. "Can't violate doctor's orders. If we do, your recovery will only take longer."

"If I don't have something to do, I'll go insane. And no recovery time will help with that."

Anatoly nodded. "I'll look for something for you to do at the office. For now, why don't you come with me to the classroom. I have a new group starting today."

Anatoly gestured to the door. "Let's go. I know teaching is not exactly your thing, but that's as much excitement as I can offer you right now."

"Better than sitting at home," Nikolai said. He wanted to get back into action as soon as possible. He was impatient, but he had to admit to himself that he wasn't ready. Physically, he was not all back yet, and the medication he had to take for another week was not helping him mentally, either.

They walked to the south end of the same hallway and into the classroom at the end of the building. The classroom was medium-sized and could comfortably fit fifteen people, which was plenty for the type of training they were receiving.

Future bodyguards, or personal protection officers, as they preferred to call themselves, needed individual attention from their instructors, and the small size of the classroom and of each class suited Anatoly just fine. The front of the classroom had a whiteboard and a rolled-up projection screen. A projector was mounted to the ceiling and connected to the computer at the instructor station at the front. The student desks were arranged in three rows, with five or six chairs in each row. The walls were bare. Anatoly considered posters, maps, slogans, and other decorative elements that many other classrooms had an unnecessary distraction and opted for clean walls painted light blue.

Nikolai found an empty seat at the back of the classroom, walked over to it, and sat down, carefully placing the cane on the floor next to his chair but out of the aisle so as not to create a tripping hazard.

The group was mainly young men who probably had just returned from the mandatory military service. Many looked like they had served in combat, Chechnya most likely. Nikolai could spot the ex-soldiers by a certain look in their eyes, despair mixed with relief. The physical and weapon training these men had was a definite advantage. The problem with the ex-soldiers was their tendency to be too aggressive and too ready to fight, and it was a challenge to convince them that a bodyguard's main task was to calculate, predict, and prevent violence. Shooting and fighting was the last resort.

Only two women were in the group. One, a dark-haired woman in khakis and a hooded sweatshirt, sat in the back. The other, a blonde with a long ponytail, black eyelashes, and bright red nails, was in the front. She did not look like a fighter, but Nikolai has learned a long time ago that looks could be, and most often were, deceptive. Women made excellent bodyguards, but not all clients realized that. Most clients still did not believe that women could be effective.

Plus, many clients were men, and their egos and images still had a hard time accepting physical help from women. But the smarter businessmen realized the advantages: women were much less obvious as bodyguards. When somebody saw a woman, they assumed she was a friend, a sister, a lover, or a nanny for the kids. Nobody instantly thought she was a bodyguard, and the surprise element made her job easier, and the client's life was safer. The blonde girl in the front definitely did not look the part, and that could work to her advantage.

Anatoly greeted the students, walked over to the podium at the front of the room, placed his notebook and phone on it, and started his lecture.

"Before you commit to this course and to the career of a bodyguard, you need to know what a bodyguard is and, even more importantly, what a bodyguard is not. A bodyguard is not a tough muscular guy armed to his teeth who wears a leather jacket and looks scary. If you are here because you like that image and want to become that image, this career is not for you. If you think a bodyguard is a person who does not care about his own life and whose job is to use his body to shield his client, it means you have been watching too many Hollywood movies. That's not what we train for and not what we do."

A young male with a shaved head raised his hand. "But that's the kind of bodyguards we always see, like at concerts, big presentations, and fancy restaurants."

Anatoly chuckled. "That's exactly the point. We always see them. Real bodyguards should not be seen. They should be gray shadows, unseen, unheard, and unnoticed. The bodyguards we see in all those places you talked about are a different category. They are more image-makers than bodyguards. If a mediocre singer, actress, or public figure wants to boost popularity, they hire a tough-looking guy to stand around and look menacing. And that often works, for the image. But as far as real protection goes, that accomplishes nothing. In the face of real danger, these image-makers can do nothing except put their clients and themselves in danger. Often, mortal danger."

"So what does a real bodyguard do?" the same student asked.

"Good question. I'll get to that." Anatoly glanced at his phone, then at Nikolai. Nikolai nodded his understanding. "Excuse me for a moment."

Anatoly walked outside and shut the classroom door behind him. The students shuffled in their seats and started chatting with each other quietly. For a few seconds, Nikolai heard Anatoly's voice and his footsteps as he walked further from the classroom. Then, everything went quiet. Nikolai sat in silence, observing the room and waiting.

A moment later, the door opened and a man in dark clothes and a ski mask rushed into the classroom, his gun drawn.

The class gasped.

"Quiet!" The man looked around the room, then pointed the gun at the young blonde woman in the front.

"Get up!" he barked. "Anyone else moves, and I'll shoot her."

The young woman stood up. Nikolai could not see her facial expression, but her posture looked cautious and collected, in control.

Nikolai shuffled in his seat, evaluating the scene. He kept his eyes on the man and the young woman, trying to hide his emotions.

With a quick movement, the young woman flipped her chair over, tripped the intruder, and applied a headlock. He fell to the floor, and two other students subdued him while she wrestled his gun away. A little unrealistic, but not bad for the first class exercise, Nikolai thought.

The classroom door opened.

"Good work, everyone!" Anatoly said from the door, then addressed the blonde woman. "Physical preparation classes were not wasted on you."

"Thanks," the woman said and sat down in her seat.

Anatoly nodded to the kidnapper. "You're free to go. Everyone else, have a seat."

He walked to the front of the classroom and addressed the young woman. "You handled this situation well. And such situations are part of our job. But our main challenge and goal as bodyguards is to do everything in our power to prevent these types of scenarios."

He paused and turned to Nikolai. "Can you take over for the remainder of class? I need to settle this one problem." He pointed to the phone. "And stop by my office once you're done here."

Nikolai picked up his cane, got up from his seat, and walked to the front of the room. "If you are here because you think that the job of a bodyguard is glamorous, because you think you will make a fortune, or because you think you will become famous, you are wrong. If that's what you expect, it would be best for you to leave now. Don't waste your time. There are plenty of other jobs out there."

He paused and looked around the room. "No shame in leaving if that's what you want to do."

Nobody moved.

Nikolai nodded, then continued. "Being a bodyguard is a dangerous job. And most of the time, it's an invisible, hidden job. The best thing you can expect at the end of the day is to keep your client alive. If you manage to keep yourself alive as well, that's an added plus. For obvious reasons."

He picked up a marker and walked to the whiteboard. "Earlier, you asked what a real bodyguard is. A real bodyguard is like a gray shadow of his client: always there, always next to the client, watching and thinking, but never intrusive. The best bodyguard is barely noticeable, barely seen, both by the clients and by their potential enemies. As for what a bodyguard does, it's three things."

Nikolai stepped closer to the board and started writing. "One is foresee a threat. Two is avoid the threat, at any cost. And if, and only if, the first two fail, then it's on to number three."

Nikolai stopped writing and looked at the class. The students were quiet and attentive, so he continued. "The third and the final task is to eliminate the threat. And if you follow these three tasks, in that order, and with a cool head, then you are likely to keep your client and yourself alive. But there are no guarantees and no certainties. Except for these two: if you stay in this job, you will develop problems with your health and problems in your personal life.

If you can't handle that certainty, you can still leave the training. You need to make the best choice that fits you and your life. Some people don't want to be constantly putting themselves in stressful and dangerous situations. Others, however, cannot imagine their life in any other way. They crave the satisfaction of a job well-done and they would rather risk their life than spend it in a regular desk job. If you are one of those people, then you've come to the right place."

Nikolai looked at the class again. The students were quiet, looking at him, and listening, probably weighing their options. He paused, allowing them to consider what he had just said. It was an important choice to make. After a pause, he continued.

"The first and foremost muscle needed for a successful bodyguard is this one."

Nikolai pointed to his head. "The brain. You need to gather information, analyze it, synthesize it, and apply it to the situation at hand. Most of the time, all of that needs to be done quickly."

Nikolai finished the lecture and dismissed the class. As the students left the room, he lingered at the desk, not wanting to show his physical vulnerabilities to the class. He remembered the time three years ago when he took the same class. Having had many of the same misconceptions about the life and work of a bodyguard, he knew exactly how these students felt. Nikolai rarely admitted it to others for fear of sounding too sentimental, but he was an idealist and wanted to make the world better. He believed that his job as a bodyguard, his ability to prevent acts of violence and save a life of a client was his small way of making this world a better and safer place.

"Great job, professor," Anatoly said when Nikolai walked back into his office.

"I could use some help in the classroom, you know. With more demand for personal protection and many new potential clients to work with, I'm having a hard time balancing teaching and client work. And the students like you."

"Thanks, but it's just not my thing. Classroom feels too confining."

"And I'm guessing you'll say the same about office work? Background checks, client interviews, things like that?"

Nikolai nodded. "Right. I don't want to do office work. Isn't there a real job I can do while I'm recuperating? I feel pretty good."

"Not now. 'Pretty good' is not good enough for our clients. Get back to 'excellent' and we'll talk again. But if you change your mind about teaching, the classroom is waiting."

"Thanks, Anatoly. You're right. I at least need to get off all those weird drugs they keep giving me. I don't feel as alert as I should be on a real assignment.

"I'll think about the classroom." Nikolai turned around and headed outside.

Chapter Two

The afternoon was fresh and crisp, rare for Moscow's usually wet winters, his leg felt better, so Nikolai started walking. The office was only three blocks away from the apartment he shared with Olga, and a walk would help clear his head and work out any lingering soreness in his body. The apartment was his, but Olga was as much in charge of it as Nikolai was. It was their joint decision to rent out Olga's place and live in Nikolai's: hers was closer to a metro station and yielded slightly higher rent, thus, more extra income for them, and his was closer to Nikolai's office. Olga's work was a few metro stations away from either one, so that was not a factor in the decision.

Living together was a new arrangement for them as of the past two months, and Nikolai knew that Olga wanted more than just a joint living arrangement, and she deserved more, too. She was caring, ambitious, successful, and pretty, and all these were qualities that any man would cherish and admire. Nikolai did, too, he just did not feel ready to completely commit to a life, marriage and kids, with Olga. He did not want her to spend her life worrying about him, or worse, becoming a widow and a single mom after an assignment gone wrong for Nikolai.

There was another issue in their relationship, too, that made it difficult for him to propose to Olga, but he did not want to admit it, even to himself.

He crossed the street and turned into a small lane leading to their building. He had lived in the center of Moscow since he was a little kid, and loved everything about it: the mix of the old and the new architecture, the narrow streets punctuated by small parks and playgrounds, the proximity to famous theatres and to the Red Square, with its beautiful red brick architecture, the ancient towers, and the newly re-opened cathedrals. He liked being close to all the important places, yet away from big streets and noise. The area and the apartment were familiar and, therefore, pleasant and comfortable.

Looking at the few remaining Soviet-style buildings, at his old school that had stayed unchanged since his childhood, and at the little bakery on the corner, Nikolai felt immersed into his own past and into the old Russia. The new Russia offered many more work and travel opportunities for him, but he sometimes felt nostalgic for the old times, for the simpler times, when he and his friends sat in the kitchen late at night, drank endless cups of tea, played their guitars, and debated the meaning of life. Now, people were different: even young people were concerned with money, business successes, purchases, and other material things. They did not seem as idealistic and as pure as Nikolai and his friends used to be.

Maybe, that kind of thinking was a sign of old age creeping slowly into Nikolai's life: the grass was greener, the snow was whiter, and everyone was better when he was young. Probably, he and his friends were just like all young people in the world are before life gets busy with work, relationships, and everyday routine. He shook off these thoughts: he was not even thirty yet, so old age was a long way from now, if he even lived to see it.

Nikolai punched in the door code, pulled open the spring-loaded front door, and entered the dark coolness of his building. For a moment, he debated walking up the stairs, but his leg was starting to ache, so he took the elevator up to the fifth floor.

The door to his apartment opened even before Nikolai could turn the key. Olga stood in the doorway, dressed in a red cocktail dress and high heels. And she looked mad.

"Olechka, are you back already?" Nikolai said.

"I'm back, and you are late." Olga sounded irritated.

"Late for what?"

"The big corporate dinner party. The one you were supposed to come with me to."

Olga shook her head dismissively, turned around and walked back inside the apartment.

Nikolai followed her. "I'm so sorry, Olechka. Of course, I'll come. When do we have to leave?"

"In fifteen minutes," she said without looking at him.

"That's plenty, and I'll drive fast." He came up to her and gently kissed her on the cheek.

"Wear something nice," Olga said, her tone softening.

Nikolai walked through the small foyer into the bedroom, took a dark suit, white shirt, and a red tie out of the closet. He placed the items on the bed and stepped into the shower.

Ten minutes later, Nikolai was in the foyer, all dressed up, clean-shaven, and ready to go. His dark curly hair was still damp from the shower, and his Makarov pistol was tucked away in the shoulder holster, away from sight. Olga used to argue with him about taking his Makarov to social functions, but has lately resorted to pretending she did not know it was there. On some things, Nikolai was not willing to compromise, and Olga learned to accept that.

Nikolai had been to many corporate events before, both with Olga and with Vasily Petrovich, in many different restaurants, but tonight's restaurant was truly spectacular. And it was not just the immaculately starched white tablecloths, the elegant arrangements of fresh flowers on each table, the crystal chandeliers, and the tasteful oil paintings on the walls that were impressive and sophisticated. What was most striking was the large picture window overlooking the entrance to the Red Square and the street below. Standing next to the window, Nikolai felt as tall as the magnificent red towers of the Kremlin, and almost as powerful. Maybe, that illusion was intentional, and that's what created the special appeal of the restaurant.

"Quite a sophisticated venue," Nikolai commented to Olga. He felt out of place among these wealthy people, men in their expensive suits and women sparkling with diamonds. Over the last few years, as he worked with the wealthiest businessmen and their partners, he had developed a distrust for most of them.

The more he learned about the way business deals were made, the less naive he was about free enterprise, at least in its Russian version.

"Do you like it here?" Olga said.

"It's spectacular," Nikolai said. There was no need to share his thoughts and spoil Olga's mood.

Olga smiled, looking perfectly comfortable. Over the last few years, she had grown accustomed to this lifestyle. Nikolai had not. She never said it to Nikolai, at least not yet, but from some of the comments she made in front of him to her friends, Nikolai was getting a distinct feeling that she needed somebody more sophisticated, more stable, somebody whose job did not involve crawling around attics and basements or dodging bullets, and somebody who could make money, more money than Nikolai, without risking his life every day. And there were plenty of available men at these corporate functions.

One such man, dressed in an elegant business suit, enveloped in a cloud of expensive cologne, and wearing a charming smile, was heading their way. He was not as tall as Nikolai but handsome and well-groomed, with broad shoulders, probably a reminder of his younger, more athletic days. Now, his most prominent feature was a mid-riff bulge under his elegant jacket, a tell-tale sign of a desk job and too much indulgence at frequent social functions. Olga rushed towards the man, pulling Nikolai with her. The man handed Olga a glass of champagne and introduced himself to Nikolai as Denis Fedorovich.

"You're lucky to have her," Denis Fedorovich said to Nikolai, and turned his attention to Olga. "We can't wait for you to start working with us. Please stop by the office on Monday afternoon, to get oriented and what not. Once the merger is complete, I will need a chief accountant. And I can't think of a better candidate than you."

Olga blushed. "I'll be happy to join you."

"And you'll be even happier when I tell you about the bonuses I'm ready to offer you." He smiled. "But enough business talk. Enjoy the evening."

Denis Fedorovich nodded to Nikolai and headed towards the buffet table.

"What's that merger he was talking about?" Nikolai said.

"He didn't tell me the details. He said he's too superstitious to say, but it sounds like a big deal. Two or three companies coming together. I'll know more soon. The merger is scheduled to be complete by the end of the month."

"You should find out the details before you agree to the job," Nikolai said.

"You have to be careful."

"You're too suspicious. Relax. It's all fine." Olga took a sip of her champagne.

"You sure you don't want to try it? It'll lighten your mood."

Another couple came up to them, making small talk and admiring Olga's dress and shoes. Nikolai pushed his thoughts about the merger aside and tried to enjoy the evening. But when they got back home and Olga started talking about how much she looked forward to her new job as the chief accountant and what a wonderful person Denis Fedorovich was, Nikolai could not hold back.

"Do you realize how dangerous this job can be for you?" Nikolai said, interrupting Olga's happy chatter and erasing the smile off her face.

"Dangerous? It's an office job. You're seeing felonies and criminals everywhere, Nikolai. You need to learn to compartmentalize."

"But you don't even know what merger he's talking about."

"What difference does it make? Mergers happen all the time, and it's just one of them. Accounting is accounting. And he's offering me more money. It's a great deal," Olga said.

"Being a chief accountant is never a great deal."

"I realize I'll have longer hours, but you have long hours, too, so what difference does that make to you?"

"It's not about the hours," Nikolai said. "If something in the books goes wrong, for any reason, the chief accountant is responsible. Prisons are filled with chief accountants who thought they were getting a great deal."

"Again? Felonies and criminals everywhere? Why can't you just support me and be happy for me, for once?" Olga glowered at him. "Good night. I hope the couch is comfortable."

When Nikolai woke up the next morning, Olga was already gone. Nikolai had always been a light sleeper, but the post-surgery medication was obviously still affecting him and his sleep. He left an apologetic message on Olga's phone, and turned on his laptop. Maybe, he could find out something about the merger that Denis Fedorovich was talking about. You could never have too much information.

He scrolled down the results pages, trying to make sense of them. Denis Fedorovich was a Board member of a large conglomerate company that operated a number of different businesses, mostly retail and telecommunications. His conglomerate also owned some construction companies, a small medical research office, an environmental consulting company, and a chain of popular toy stores.

It was unlikely that there was going to be a true merger. Most likely, another acquisition of a company in one of these fields. And if the deal had not been finalized, it made sense that Denis Fedorovich did not want to give the details to Olga.

Nikolai pushed his laptop aside and got up. That search was pointless. He would not find any information that would convince Olga not to accept the job offer.

Nikolai rolled out his yoga mat and started doing physical therapy exercises that he was taught in the hospital. He needed to recover.

A few minutes into his stretches, Nikolai's phone buzzed.

"You're in luck, professor," he heard Anatoly's voice. "I got an easy assignment for you. Can you be here in an hour?"

"Of course."

Fifty-five minutes later, Nikolai, dressed in jeans, heavy boots, and a winter jacket that easily concealed his shoulder holster, walked into Anatoly's office.

Anatoly was at his desk, dressed in his white karate uniform. His black belt hung on the coat rack in the corner.

"New dress code?" Nikolai said.

"This client was a last minute thing, and I got a karate class to teach. But don't worry, I changed into the uniform after I called you. The client had already left by then," Anatoly said. "Have a seat."

Nikolai leaned his cane against the wall and sat down across from Anatoly.

"From what I can tell," Anatoly said, "it's a case of an overprotective dad who's worried that something bad will happen to his young daughter or that she'll get in trouble once she's away from home."

"How young are we talking about? A child? He's concerned about kidnapping?"

"No, nothing like that. The girl is twenty-two but sounds immature and prone to bad decisions. And dad can't control what she does anymore," Anatoly said.

"And how can I help with that?"

"How would you like to get away for a while?" Anatoly said.

"Olga would like me to, no doubt," Nikolai said.

Anatoly kept his gaze on Nikolai. "Are things okay? Is there anything I need to know?"

"As okay as they have been lately," Nikolai said. "Some time apart will be good for both of us. So, how far are we talking about?"

"A couple of hours by plane. Your client is going to a small town in Komi Republic to work as an interpreter for an oil company."

"An interpreter of what?"

"A Russian-English interpreter. She has a linguistics degree and impressive experience from what I'm told, despite her young age, so the company hired her right away. It's a joint company with the Canadians. She'll be working with the director of the company."

"And that's her first job? Sounds pretty high-level."

"First job away from home, lots of short-term free-lance assignments in Moscow. Most Moscow interpreters don't want to travel to a small town that far north, but she's adventurous enough to want to go."

"Or desperate to get away from her overprotective father?"

"That's possible, too." Anatoly nodded.

"How far north are we talking about? Siberia north?" Nikolai asked.

"Farther." Anatoly got up, pushed his chair back in, and turned to the large map on the wall behind his desk. He circled a large area northeast of Moscow. "This is Siberia." He traced a line straight up on the map. "This is Komi Republic."

Nikolai followed the line with his eyes. Komi Republic was further north than he had thought.

Anatoly glanced at Nikolai, then moved his finger up on the map, all the way to the Arctic Circle. "And this is Upper Luzinsk."

Nikolai shook his head. "She must like the arctic cold weather and remote places."

Anatoly did not respond. He simply turned back to his desk, sat down and looked straight at Nikolai, probably expecting him to say something else.

"What's my role exactly?" Nikolai said. "What am I protecting her from?"

"Not much, and I don't see much danger there, to anyone, so mainly your job is to demonstrate that she has a bodyguard, a chaperone of sorts. Contrary to what we usually do, feel free to tell everyone you're her bodyguard. I think that's what the dad wants. That way, nobody will mess with her. No dubious boyfriends or married guys looking for adventures. Are you good with that?"

"Do I have a choice?"

"You could stay at home and recuperate."

"I'm going to Komi," Nikolai said.

"Good answer," Anatoly said. "I know it's more of a babysitting assignment than a real one, but you need time to

30

recuperate. Nevertheless, I'm taking it seriously, and so should you."

"Of course. A job is a job. Tell me more about her and her family," Nikolai said.

"Her dad worked abroad for many years, which means he was making decent money even when she was still little. They lived all over Europe, but mainly in Germany."

"What did he do?"

"Trade attaché for the Russian embassy," Anatoly said.

"I see," Nikolai said. "Does he still work for the government?"

"Not anymore. As soon as they got back to Moscow, he left his job, got into the banking business and made some serious money. And, like many people who suddenly became rich, he lost his head."

"Can you elaborate?" Nikolai asked.

"Fancy cars, exotic vacations, that kind of thing. But that wasn't the problem. The problem was that he was always raising his daughter like a princess, and the new wealth made him want to spoil her even more. He bought her anything and everything she wanted, and that ruined their relationship. She started seeing him as a source of new fancy things and easy money, nothing more. Not my words, his."

"Where's the mom?" Nikolai said.

"That's another problem in that relationship. Her mom died when the girl was very young. The dad never remarried and devoted his whole life to his daughter. His way to make up for the loss of her mom was to spend more and more money on the daughter. Good intentions, and we know where they lead. Now, he's worried that she'll go wild as soon as she's on her own for the first time. She graduated from college last spring, and this will be her first job away from home," Anatoly said.

"Got it. What does the dad do now? Any background on him?" Nikolai said.

"Any background? No. Complete background? Yes. He's a banker. Quite successful. Nothing fishy in his business. Other questions?" Anatoly said.

"No. The task is clear. Keep the girl out of trouble. Not too exciting but better than sitting at home," Nikolai said.

"Excellent. You're on the charter flight tomorrow. Here's all the information."

Anatoly handed Nikolai a printed page. "The dad and the girl will be at the airport. She's Natalya Abramova. Dad's name is Konstantin."

Early next morning, Nikolai woke up alone. Olga had spent the night at her parents', at least according to the curt message she left on his phone. Nikolai wrote a long apologetic note, attached it to a bouquet of flowers, and dropped both off at Olga's office on his way to the airport.

When he got to the charter flights terminal, he spotted Natalya and her dad immediately. In the crowd dressed in long thick pants, big boots, heavy parkas, and carrying drab-looking luggage, Natalya in her expensive mink coat and her dad holding two Louis Vuitton suitcases stood out. Natalya was tall and slender, with an unruly mane of red hair showing from under her fur hat.

Nikolai came up to them. "Natalya and Konstantin?"

Konstantin, a middle-aged man with tired eyes, greeted him politely and shook his hand.

"Ah, the bodyguard," Natalya said. "Can you help?" She pointed to two bags on the ground next to her.

Nikolai picked up one bag with his left hand. His own luggage consisted of an old backpack and a duffel bag slung over his shoulder.

"And this?" She pointed to the other one.

"Sorry. It's yours to carry. My right hand always needs to be free."

She chuckled. "In case somebody starts firing?"

"Exactly. Let's go." Nikolai pointed towards the airport checkpoint.

Natalya huffed, picked up the other bag, and started walking. Nikolai and Konstantin followed a few steps behind her.

"She's trouble," Konstantin said. "I don't envy you. I've spoiled her and now can't get any control back. Maybe, this job will be good for her. She needs to feel responsible for something. Anything."

They checked in their larger bags and came up to a checkpoint where a uniformed officer checked off their names on the passenger list. There were no metal detectors and no x-ray machines, just an officer with a clipboard.

"Need our passports?" Nikolai asked.

The officer shook his head. "It's a charter flight. Your names are on the list. That's all that matters. Have a good flight."

"You never check passports?" Nikolai asked.

The guard shrugged. "Why check? Nothing bad has happened yet. And charter flights are always safe."

Nikolai patted his pocket, feeling the extra cartridge for his Makarov. "As you say."

Natalya waved good-bye to her dad. No kisses, no hugs, and no attempts for either from her or the dad. Nikolai sighed. She must be real trouble for the dad. He seemed relieved to have handed her over to Nikolai.

They walked down the hallway, then out onto the tarmac, and climbed into a small van that took them to a far corner of the airfield where a YAK-40 plane was waiting for them. Nikolai had flown in enough of them to know that they were not the best of what Soviet aviation industry could produce, but because of their compact size and ability to land in small airports, YAK-40 planes were a popular choice for charter flights to remote areas.

They entered the plane through a narrow ladder in the back and walked into the cabin lined with two rows of seats on each side.

"Take the window seat," Nikolai said.

"Thanks. You're such a gentleman," Natalya said. "Are you that nice to all your women?"

"Let's establish something once and for all. You are not my woman. You're a client. I'm your bodyguard. That's the extent of our relationship. No more and no less."

"For now," Natalya said.

"Yes, for now. Until the mission is over. No relationship whatsoever after that. Please keep that in mind."

Nikolai knew he sounded a little harsh, but he wanted Natalya to know the limits from the very beginning. Later on, he would need to talk to her more, get to know her better, and help them both develop trust in each other. With other clients, that was the first step. With Natalya, considering the nature of this assignment, her personality and her history, that would have to wait. Maintaining a distance was more important right now.

"Champagne?" The flight attendant, a short young brunette, came up to them with a tray filled with champagne flutes.

"I'll take one." Natalya grabbed a glass.

"None for me, thanks," Nikolai said.

"You're so perfect. You don't drink, you don't smoke, you don't swear." She took a sip of her champagne. "It's delicious."

"I don't drink while on duty."

"But you must have some vices. What are they? Can I help you find them?" Natalya smiled mischievously, put her glass on the tray table in front of her and turned to Nikolai.

"None. I'm perfect. You just said it yourself."

"Too bad," Natalya said. "I hope you change your mind. And not about the champagne." She turned her head to Nikolai and leaned towards him, her face inches away from his.

The intercom buzzed, followed by an announcement to fasten seatbelts. Natalya leaned away from Nikolai and reached for her seatbelt. Nikolai reached for his.

A moment later, with a jerk, the plane started taxiing and gaining speed. Soon, it reached the end of the runway and lifted off into the cloudy milky sky. Soon, Moscow disappeared behind a thick white blanket.

As it attempted to reach the cruising altitude, the small plane trembled and shook. The engines whined like a wounded seal. With each twist, tremble, and whine of the plane, Natalya grabbed his arm and whimpered, "Are we going to die, Mr. Bodyguard?"

"We'll be just fine. Turbulence is not unusual. Just relax."

It will be a long assignment, Nikolai thought as he tried to unclutch Natalya from his arm. He had forgotten how immature twenty-two-year-olds could be, and Natalya was at the top of that list. No wonder her dad barely said bye. He was probably relieved to get her off his hands for a while.

As the airplane gained altitude, it stopped shaking and dipping, and the engines went from pained whining to a dull roar. The flight attendant brought more champagne. Natalya

35

took another glass, retrieved a glossy magazine from her purse, and started leafing through it. Soon, she was fast asleep. Nikolai got out a paperback mystery he brought along and started reading.

After two hours of the flight, cabin lights dimmed, and the engines started their high-pitch whining again. The change in the cabin woke up Natalya. She opened her eyes and looked at Nikolai, then out the window.

The airplane dropped altitude, broke through thick clouds, and lunged towards the grayish white ground below.

"Please fasten your seat belts and prepare for landing in Upper Luzinsk International Airport," the flight attendant said through the intercom.

"International?" Natalya said to Nikolai. "Look at that."

A dimly lit weathered shack with hardly discernible letters "Upper Luzinsk" decorated the end of a lonely runway. Nikolai could not see any other buildings in the twilight, just boundless snow and ice. The plane screeched to a stop, and cabin lights flickered back on.

"Local time is half past ten in the morning. Welcome to Upper Luzinsk," the flight attendant said.

As passengers around them jumped up from their seats, Nikolai grabbed his bag and followed Natalya to the back of the airplane. Passengers in front of them were cautiously walking down a small shaky ramp.

"It looks slippery," Natalya said.

"Hold on to the rail," Nikolai said. "With your free hand. Put your bag strap over your shoulder." No matter how much she whined, he was not going to let her turn him into a porter.

As Nikolai took the first step out of the airplane, a blast of cold air hit him in the face. In front of him, Natalya lost her footing and slipped. Nikolai grabbed her to stop her from falling.

"Thank you, Mr. Bodyguard. You're so strong," Natalya said.

"Watch your step, please."

"You can pick up your bags in the loading zone of the airfield," the flight attendant said and pointed to a fenced-in area where an open-bed truck stood loaded with suitcases.

The air and the ground were so cold that Nikolai felt like he was barefoot. With every step, the cold from the ground radiated up through the thin soles of his boots intended for a much milder Moscow winter. He kept walking on the airfield next to Natalya, his wounded leg aching with each step, probably from the cold weather.

"Welcome to Upper Luzinsk," yelled a man in a parka from the top of the baggage pile. He motioned for the passengers to walk off the airfield through the small iron gate. "I'll throw all the bags over the fence; it's much faster that way.

If you try to find your own bags in the pile, it will take too long. We'll all freeze here."

Natalya gasped, probably horrified at the thought of her fancy suitcases being thrown over a shabby fence onto the freezing ground. Nikolai tightened his scarf and stepped up to the fence.

A tall man in scuffed-up boots and a thick winter coat, handmade woolen scarf wrapped tightly around his neck, came up to them. He was thin and looked to be in his late twenties or early thirties. "I'll catch your bags," he said. "Where to? I'll drive you." He pointed to his snow-covered rusty Lada. "Not fancy, but the heater is working. My name's Oleg."

"The main square," Nikolai answered, each word accompanied by thick white vapor.

Brushing the snowflakes off her face, Natalya stood shivering next to him. Her eyes were watering from the cold and her nose running.

"First time here? Jump into the car. You're lucky it's a warm spell. Much easier to get used to this place if you're not hit with the real cold right away," Oleg said, rubbing his red weathered hands together and stomping his feet.

Nikolai wondered what the real cold felt like as he watched their fellow passengers, all dressed in bulky coats and boots, scurry around the ramshackle airport building, load their suitcases and bags into rusty cars, and venture into the icy and snowy twilight of Upper Luzinsk.

Oleg threw the bags in the trunk. "Luzinsk Oil, right?"

"How did you know where we are going?" Natalya asked Oleg when they were inside the car.

"Not too hard to guess. Luzinsk Oil has been hiring a lot of people lately. And that's the only real oil company in town. There's also Luna Oil and Gas, but they are a much smaller operation. There was talk of expanding and new hires, but not much movement in that direction so far." Oleg steered the car out of the small parking lot and onto the only road to town.

"Who owns Luna Oil?" Nikolai asked.

"I don't know," Oleg said. "They've been bought and sold so many times, it's hard to keep track. And they don't have nearly as many computers as Luzinsk Oil. As I said, it's a much smaller operation."

"How do you know how many computers they have?" Nikolai said.

"I do a little bit of computer work for both companies."

"And you drive, too?" Nikolai said.

"Sure. I run errands for anybody who's willing to pay me. I'm not too proud to make money any way I can. We need it now that my wife can't work anymore."

"What's wrong with her?" Natalya asked. "Is she sick?"

"No, no," Oleg said. "She's pregnant. I can't wait to become a dad. And when I make enough money, I want to buy a small place down south, maybe even on the Black Sea. Young kids should not live in this harsh climate."

Nobody should live in this harsh climate, thought Nikolai.

Chapter Three

The narrow road leading from the airport into town was surrounded by vast open space from horizon to colorless horizon. Low rays of the hazy sun lit up a grayish-white sky. Vegetation was sparse: lining the road were dwarf pine trees barely visible behind snowdrifts, as if nature itself objected to being here, in this unforgiving climate that offered nothing to any living creatures. The only reason anybody would ever move to this desolate area was the allure of the wealth promised by the oil field. Some got that wealth and moved away, but most stayed and kept working, insufficient income or other life circumstances prohibiting them from finding a more hospitable place to live.

Along the edge of the road, electric posts were stuck in the ground at random angles. Not a single one pointed straight up. Many almost crossed each other, and from a distance created an image of a gigantic surreal cemetery peppered with misshapen crosses.

"These posts are so crooked," Natalya said.

"It's the permafrost," Oleg said. "When the top layer melts, the trees and posts lose their grounding and lean. When it freezes again, they freeze, too, right where they've leaned."

"I've never seen that before," Natalya said.

"You'll see lots of things here you've never seen before," Oleg said. His Lada turned the corner, but the white and desolate landscape around them did not change. "Just a few more minutes till the main square. You'll be working for a very good company, by the way. Pyotr Alekseevich is great."

"Pyotr Alekseevich?" Nikolai asked.

"He's the new director. Everyone in town knows him and loves him. He used to be the mayor but left that job to head Luzinsk Oil."

"More money?" Nikolai asked. "The so-called public service doesn't pay much?"

Oleg shook his head. "Nothing like that. He didn't even want to head the company, but was left with no choice."

"No choice? Why is that?" Nikolai asked.

"He was the only one who could save the company. Things are still not quite settled, but I hear the deal is in the making. It should be signed at the Board meeting in a week or so. The whole town will be partying when that happens."

"You know a lot about the company," Nikolai said.

"Everyone here does," Oleg said. "Oil and gas is our only industry, and it defines how we all live. The previous director did not last long, and we were all relieved when he left."

"Who was the previous director?" Nikolai asked.

"Some bureaucrat from Moscow who only cared about money and his own profit. He didn't even pay corporate taxes, and that's what started this whole mess. Anyway, you'll hear plenty from Pyotr Alekseevich. It's on everyone's mind now."

Nikolai turned to the window. The main road, open to the brutal arctic gale, created a sort of a wind tunnel, and Nikolai could hear the wind whistling around them.

The landscape changed suddenly, replacing the white emptiness with block buildings that varied in height from two to about ten stories. They were definitely in the urban area now. In the dim light of the arctic morning, Nikolai glimpsed a typical two-story school structure inside a cluster of apartment buildings, probably placed there to provide the children some protection from the scything wind. Like many hastily built towns, Upper Luzinsk had no suburban areas, no villages surrounding it. Just the tundra and the center of town in the middle of it, if it could even be called a town. Nikolai did not see a single restaurant, cafe, sports club, or a church around. A place without a soul.

Oleg slowed down at a small intersection to let a middle-aged couple, holding on to each other, cross the street. The couple were the first people Nikolai saw in this town. It was not surprising: not many would want to venture outside in this cold weather. Small streets crossed the main road and disappeared into the sparse tundra and the white hills behind it. The center of town was within walking distance from its furthest edge.

"How old is this town?" Nikolai asked.

"Construction started in the 1960's and 1970's when major oil reserves were found. The climate here is not suitable for living, and neither are most of these buildings. The construction was quick and sloppy."

Nikolai nodded. He didn't want to offend Oleg but the town looked drab and depressing. Unlike older towns that grew out of people's desire to live in them because of their mild climate, proximity to ports, or other attractive natural features, the construction of Upper Luzinsk was mandated by the government for the sole purpose of oil production, a purpose that was clearly stated in enormous letters above the tallest building, a six-story apartment block, "Let's produce more oil for the motherland."

The only other architectural addition to the soulless architecture were huge red, pink, and yellow triangles painted on all apartment buildings. The single attraction in this vast frozen area was oil, and it was obviously strong enough to build a town around it.

"These buildings look ugly," Natalya said.

"Nobody cared about looks when this town was built. It was all about oil production," Oleg said. "Upper Luzinsk is the oil capital of the Russian north, or so we are told."

"But still. Just look at those triangles. Do people here have no taste?" Natalya said. "How tacky."

"Stay here for a while, and then we'll talk about taste," Oleg said. "With the drab and dreary endless days of winter with barely any daylight for months, you would pick up a bucket of bright paint yourself."

Nikolai doubted Natalya was the type to pick up anything herself, but he was pretty confident she was the type who did not like to get bored or stay bored. The question was what exactly she would do to keep herself entertained in this small quiet town, and how Nikolai would be able to prevent her from entertaining herself in ways that her dad would not find appropriate.

"What's going on there?" Natalya said.

Nikolai turned to see what she was looking at. Oleg slowed down as they drove by an apartment building, its entrance surrounded by police cars with flashing lights and an ambulance. A small crowd gathered in front of the building, huddling together. Two paramedics carried a stretcher out of the building and set it on the frozen ground.

"This person must be dead. They wouldn't just leave a living patient on the ground, would they?" Natalya said.

"Must be dead," Oleg said.

"What do you think happened?" Natalya said.

"Probably a heart attack," Oleg said.

"And that's why the police are here?" Nikolai said.

"I don't know what's going on. I'm here with you, not out there," Oleg said. "It's just a guess."

Nikolai did not ask anything else, and neither did Natalya. The dead body on the stretcher could be the result of many tragic but not necessarily unexpected circumstances, including a heart attack, so the police and medical presence was not a bad thing. At least this town had the police and medical services, as well as a way to ensure they showed up. However, something about the scene, besides the police cars, told Nikolai that the reason for the presence was not a heart attack. The people gathered by the building looked too distraught and too oblivious to the brutal cold. Even from the inside of Oleg's Lada, Nikolai could sense their fear. It was not a heart attack that made these people stand outside, many with their coats unbuttoned and no hats. Whatever had happened in that building was something more serious and much more sinister.

Oleg turned the corner, and the building, with its distraught inhabitants, disappeared from view.

"Almost there." Oleg pulled over to a gray three-storied building with large snow sculptures of alligators, monkeys, and elephants in front of it.

Nikolai wondered if placing exotic animals from tropical climates in the midst of this arctic town was another way its inhabitants tried to cheer themselves up.

"This is Upper Luzinsk for you," Oleg said.

"That's the center of town?" Natalya said.

"As central as it gets," Oleg said. "But that's not the compound. I just need to pick up some papers so we can get you settled in the hotel." Probably catching Nikolai's questioning glance, Oleg quickly added, "Don't worry. I know the routine. It's not the first time I pick up Moscow employees here. I'll be right back."

Oleg left the car running, with the heater on, and jumped out. He strode inside the building and came back a few minutes later with a thick envelope.

"All done," he said as he sat back behind the wheel, his tone quickly changing from casual to business-like. Oleg was no longer a driver, he was a company employee with a job to do, and his words clearly reflected that.

"Let's go to the compound," Oleg said. "How long are you staying for, by the way? Most interpreters stay for four weeks, that's the typical shift. They work every day, weekends included, from seven in the morning till seven at night. All meals are provided, and the restaurant is inside the compound. And that's a good thing, since the stores here have nothing. Are you okay sharing a room in the hotel with other interpreters? Or do you want private rooms?"

"Natalya and I will share a room," Nikolai asked.

"What?" Natalya said. "I'm not sharing a room with you."

"A lovers' quarrel, I see." Oleg chuckled. "None of my business, so you two figure out what you want to do."

"I want my own room," Natalya said.

"That's not happening," Nikolai said. "And not for the reasons you're thinking about. As I told you before, I am not interested in you. This living arrangement is purely for your safety. If you want your own room, I'll be happy to take you back to your dad's house," Nikolai said and addressed Oleg. "I'm Natalya's bodyguard, and I need to be with her. Does the hotel have suites?" It felt awkward to introduce himself as a bodyguard, but that's what Natalya's dad apparently wanted.

"Bodyguard, really?" Oleg said. "Come on, you two can be honest with me. I don't care who shares rooms with whom or what goes on in the hotel. Just get the work done."

"It's true." Nikolai reached into his pocket and showed Oleg his ID card issued by the agency.

For a moment, Oleg took his eyes off the road and glanced at the card, then at Nikolai, his expression registering surprise. "So, you really aren't kidding?"

Oleg glanced at Natalya in the rear-view mirror. "Why do you need a bodyguard?"

"Ask my dad."

"Sorry, none of my business," Oleg said. "Either way, you can share a room."

"Only if it's a suite," Natalya said.

"That can be arranged," Oleg said. "Here we are. That's the compound."

His Lada came to the edge of a large corner lot with a dozen of identical manufactured office buildings, most of them two stories, and all of them white.

The buildings were huddled around an older, taller structure that looked like a typical Soviet-style apartment building. The whole compound was surrounded by a chain-link fence.

"Is this fence new?" Nikolai asked Oleg.

"It is. How did you know?"

"No snow on the ground on either side of it. You would have to clear away the snow to put the posts in, and it snows often here, so the ground would not stay exposed for long. Uneven distances between the posts shows me that it was put up in a hurry. Any special reason for building it?"

"Built last week after stacks of concrete blocks and pipes disappeared while we were all having lunch. It's a temporary fence. We'll need a better one eventually."

"Did they find out who stole it?" Natalya asked.

"No," Oleg said. "It's pretty much impossible. And there's the hotel, by the way. Not exactly five stars." Oleg pointed to the old Soviet-style structure that Nikolai noticed earlier. Its paint was peeling, and it looked out of place in this modern compound. "Luzinsk Oil didn't build it, as you can probably tell. It belongs to the town, but Luzinsk Oil is leasing this lot, and the hotel was the only building on it, so they ended up leasing the whole hotel, too. It was the easiest way to work out the lease agreement with the city."

Oleg pulled over to the gated entrance, stopped, and pushed the intercom button. The entrance gate was tall and massive, a stark contrast to the flimsy chain-link fence.

"Any firearms in the car?" a voice said through the intercom.

Oleg turned to Natalya and Nikolai. "Firearms?"

"I don't have any firearms, but Nikolai probably does," Natalya said.

"Yes, I do," Nikolai said.

"Wait, please," the intercom said. "I need to talk to you."

A few moments later, a middle-aged dark-haired man in a parka came out of the gate and approached their car. Nikolai stepped outside, the bitter cold hitting him at once and making his eyes water.

The man came up to the car, took the mitten off his right hand and extended his hand to Nikolai. "I'm Vanya, the security director. Are you the new interpreter for Pyotr Alekseevich?"

Nikolai shook his hand, Vanya's handshake strong and confident. "Not me. Natalya is the interpreter. I'm her bodyguard."

"Bodyguard?" Vanya pulled his mitten back on and started walking towards the small security building by the gate, packed snow crunching with each step. He motioned for Nikolai to follow him. "What is she, a rock star?"

"No. She just has an overprotective father."

Vanya shook his head. "A bodyguard. That's new. There's always something with these Moscow interpreters: the hotel is not good enough, the weather is too cold, or the food is too greasy, but this is new. A bodyguard." He chuckled.

Nikolai shrugged. "I did not make the decision to come here, but a job is a job."

"And you have firearms?"

"Yes."

"What kind?"

"Two Makarov pistols."

They stopped at the door with an Employees Only sign on it. Vanya reached for the doorknob. "You have to leave your firearms with me in the security office.

No weapons are allowed at the compound." He pulled on the doorknob.

Nikolai did not move. "Can't do that. No firearms, no interpreter."

"Not my problem," Vanya said.

"It will be your problem if your boss finds out."

Vanya shook his head again. "Let me call Pyotr Alekseevich."

Still shaking his head and muttering something under his breath, Vanya motioned for Nikolai to get back into the car and stepped into the security office.

"Trouble already, Mr. Bodyguard?" Natalya said when Nikolai sat down next to her.

"Nothing that can't be resolved with a call to the boss, I'm sure," Nikolai said.

Oleg was quiet, suddenly busy with his phone.

A few moments later, the intercom buzzed. Oleg put his phone down, lowered the window and pushed the intercom button.

"You all can go in," Vanya's voice crackled through the intercom. "Just tell Nikolai to keep his firearms out of sight."

"Will do," Nikolai said, fighting the temptation to comment on this obvious request.

After a short drive inside the compound, Oleg pulled over to a curb, or at least to where the curb would have been if it were not for the tall wall of firmly packed snow that separated the sidewalk from the street. He led Natalya and Nikolai towards one of the buildings. The heat enveloped them as soon as they stepped inside. Nikolai took his hat off, pulled off his gloves, and stuffed them in his pockets.

The inside of the building was all business, with industrial gray carpet, no-nonsense track lighting, and imitation wood panels on the walls. The only element that felt non-utilitarian were the curtains, with bright multicolored geometric patterns on them.

"The conference room is down here," Oleg said pointing down the hallway. "And Pyotr Alekseevich's office is upstairs."

They walked up to the second floor and down a narrow hallway to the door at the end. Oleg half-knocked on the door and immediately pushed it open.

The office was small and cluttered, not what Nikolai had expected the director of an oil company to have. No mahogany-style desks, fancy furnishings, or crystal chandeliers here. Just like the rest of the building, the room was all business-like and simple, like a field operations office. Both walls were lined with desks, with shelves hanging above the desks. The desk nearest to the door had a computer on it, the others were piled high with books and papers. The office was so filled with things that Nikolai could barely see its occupant, a man in a fuzzy gray sweater, dark pants, and big winter boots. His head was topped with an unruly mane of salt-and-pepper hair. A large moustache hid the top of his mouth. The man pushed aside the papers on his desk and got up.

"Welcome to the north," he said to Nikolai and Natalya. "I'm Pyotr Alekseevich."

He smiled, shook hands with them, then turned to Oleg. "If it's not too much trouble, could you take their bags to the hotel? I'd like to get right down to business. And when you get a chance, could you do your magic?" He pointed to the computer on the desk next to the door. "It's slow again."

"Sure thing, Pyotr Alekseevich. I can come back tonight, after you're done here," Oleg said.

"If you don't mind working late."

"Not at all."

After Oleg left, Pyotr Alekseevich pulled an electric kettle off a shelf, filled it with water from a large pitcher on his desk, and pointed to the two chairs across from his desk. "Have a seat." He sat down himself, reached into a desk drawer and put three large green ceramic mugs on his desk. "We'll have some tea and chat. I'll bring you up to date on the happenings here."

"You are going to stay here, aren't you?" Pyotr Alekseevich addressed Natalya. "The previous interpreter escaped after a week: too cold and too stressful. We can't do much without good interpreters, and none of us, Canadians or Russians, have worked with interpreters before. It takes patience. From everybody."

"I'll stay," Natalya said.

"Good," Pyotr Alekseevich said.

The kettle clicked off, and Pyotr Alekseevich put a teabag in each mug and poured the water into the mugs. He handed one cup to Natalya and turned to Nikolai. "I realize that one of the conditions of Natalya's employment was that she brings a bodyguard with her. This is really odd for me, but I agreed because right now, especially before the Board meeting, I really need a good interpreter, and Natalya came highly recommended. I have no idea how this whole bodyguard thing works. I've only seen it in movies. So please tell me, Nikolai."

"You can ignore me for the most part. I'll tag along with Natalya to wherever she needs to be."

Pyotr Alekseevich picked up his mug and took a sip of the hot liquid. "You mean to all the meetings and briefings and trips to the oil field?"

"Yes," Nikolai said.

"And what are you going to do there? Some meetings can last a long time."

"Don't worry about it. My job is to make sure that Natalya is protected, and the length of a meeting is not a factor in it."

"I still don't understand. Why is this protection even needed? Neither her dad nor your boss could explain it to me. What could possibly happen to her during a meeting?"

"Probably, nothing. But I was hired to protect her, and I will do my job the best I can, whether an obvious threat is present or not. Also, if I see something I need to discuss with you, I will let you know."

"Like what?" Pyotr Alekseevich said.

"I don't know right now, but that's what I'm supposed to look for. And I won't be in the way, if that's a concern for you. I'll be quiet and unobtrusive."

"All right, fine," Pyotr Alekseevich said to Nikolai and turned to Natalya.

"Tomorrow morning, we have a pipeline meeting up on the oil field. The discussion can get pretty involved and quite technical, and I'd like you to be able to follow it." Pyotr Alekseevich reached for the keyboard, then shook his head. "Sorry. My computer has been acting up today. Let's do this the old-fashioned way." He unfolded a map on top of a pile of books, notepads and empty coffee mugs cluttering his desk, reached under the map and pulled out a pencil. "Here's our oil field." He drew a circle in the middle of the map.

"Here's the river." He drew a line next to the circle.

Natalya seemed to be listening carefully as Pyotr Alekseevich talked about the layout of the field, the problems of delivering construction materials across the permafrost zone that melted over the brief summer months, the urgency of replacing some old sections of the pipeline, and the upcoming tender to find an environmental consulting company. It all made sense to Nikolai, but what did not make any sense at all was his own assignment. There seemed to be no need for his services, no danger for Natalya, and no opportunities for wild partying that her dad might have been concerned about. Upper Luzinsk was as isolated, quiet, and uneventful as a small town could be.

Chapter Four

While Pyotr Alekseevich and Natalya were talking, Nikolai stepped outside and looked around. Pyotr Alekseevich's office building was in the center of the compound of manufactured buildings, all placed within walking distance of each other on a large lot. The buildings were connected by walkways made out of packed snow and lit day and night by dim street lamps. Bright spotlights illuminated all entrances, probably to help employees find their way into the heated buildings through darkness and blizzards. In this climate, hypothermia would set in quickly.

The front end of the compound, with the main gate and the security building, felt like it was in the middle of town, at the intersection of Upper Luzinsk's main thoroughfare, a two-lane narrow road leading to the airport, and a smaller street. The rear of the compound bordered the frozen tundra. The town was so small that it would probably take a brisk fifteen-minute walk to get from the central square to the wilderness of the tundra.

A gust of icy wind enveloped Nikolai in a flurry of thick snowflakes. He shook them off, pulled his scarf tighter, and kept walking. He left his cane in Moscow as he no longer needed it, but he could definitely feel the ache in his leg now. He hoped that it would go away as his body adjusted to the extreme cold.

The chain-link fence around the buildings was barely taller than Nikolai, not much higher than two meters. Nikolai could not spot any security cameras, or any other indications that safety had ever been on anybody's mind in this desolate little town. He surveyed the white landscape, the line of the horizon lost somewhere between the snow and the sky, then headed towards the gate and the security office. It was time to talk to Vanya.

Nikolai knocked on the door of the security office marked with the familiar *Employees Only* sign.

"Come in!" he heard Vanya's voice.

Nikolai turned the knob and stepped inside. A lone security monitor, no image visible on it, hung on the wall above a desk cluttered with newspapers and teacups. More security monitors, their screens blank, were on the desk itself. A small cot stood in the corner. The intercom system was mounted next to the door.

A flashlight hung on a nail to the left of the intercom system.

Vanya sat at the far end of the room at a small table holding a pencil in his right hand. A newspaper with a large crossword puzzle was spread out in front of him. Vanya nodded to Nikolai and gestured for him to sit down.

"Greetings, Vanya," Nikolai said. He sat down on a rickety chair across the table from Vanya. "How's the puzzle coming along?"

"Not bad if you like Shakespeare, and I do. Is that what you came here for? To help me with the crossword puzzle?"

"I need to talk to you."

"I gathered that much," Vanya said. "About what? Your weapons again? It's between you and Pyotr Alekseevich now."

"No, not the weapons," Nikolai said.

"Then what? Not about last night's incident, I hope." Vanya looked up from the puzzle and tapped his pencil on the side of the table.

"What incident?" Nikolai said.

"You know, the dead man," Vanya said. "Oleg said you saw it, too."

"The dead man at the apartment building?"

Vanya nodded. "Yes, the one and only. Everyone wants to talk about it: the local detectives, the Moscow detectives, even the federal investigators. And I already told them all that I know. I really have nothing else to say about it, and I don't understand all the fuss about it. Much Ado about Nothing, just like number six down." Vanya filled in a few boxes and looked up.

"I haven't heard what you make of it, so why don't you tell me," Nikolai said.

"I gather it wasn't a heart attack."

Vanya hesitated, then put down his pencil and looked at Nikolai. "Not much to tell. Nothing like that had ever happened before. We're a small and quiet town, but freak accidents and events can happen anywhere, right?"

"Just tell me what you think happened," Nikolai said.

"Jealous rage, nothing else," Vanya said. "It's too bad a man had to die over it, but husbands can be jealous."

"He was involved with a married woman and the husband killed him?"

"That's right. A tragedy of Shakespearean proportions." Vanya glanced at the crossword puzzle, grabbed an eraser from his desk and rubbed it on the newspaper, erasing something.

"You like Shakespeare?" Nikolai asked, pointing to a large weathered volume on Vanya's desk.

"Who doesn't? That guy knew real drama and really understood people," Vanya said. "And this newspaper likes to publish crosswords with clues about Shakespeare, so I use the book to look things up once in a while."

"Doing an Internet search is faster," Nikolai said.

Vanya shook his head. "That would be cheating. Looking through the book is more honest."

"Did the police find the killer?" Nikolai asked.

"Still looking," Vanya said. "He fled town together with his wife. I guess he must have forgiven her."

"Do you know any of the three?"

"Sure. Everyone knows everyone here. The girl is a hairdresser, moved here from the fishing village up north when she got married. That was probably two or three years ago. Her husband, Mikhail, applied to work security for us one time, but never got hired."

"Why not? Any problems?"

"Not that I know of. Mikhail was a little late in applying. The pay is good here, better than anywhere else in town, so the positions filled right away. And that was just fine with me. I never liked him too much."

"Why not?" Nikolai asked.

"I don't know. Just didn't like him. Can't really explain it. But leave it to the police. That's in the past as far as our company is concerned." Vanya opened his Shakespeare book, looked through it, picked up the pencil, and filled in one more line of the crossword puzzle.

"I hope so," Nikolai said. "Are you sure there was nothing else behind the murder? No other motive?"

"What else would there be?" Vanya shrugged. "Just relax a little. This is not Moscow. We lead a simple life here. No contract murders, no exploding buildings, no fatal poisonings. Women are a scarce commodity here, and what happened is a result of it. Two men, one woman. Tragic ending. Just like Othello and Desdemona." Vanya looked down at the crossword again. "And what was the other guy's name, the one that Desdemona supposedly had an affair with?"

"Cassio?" Nikolai said.

Vanya checked the puzzle. "Right. That fits." He wrote it down and looked up at Nikolai. "So, that's exactly what happened. Desdemona the hairdresser had an affair

56

with Cassio the security guard, and Othello-Mikhail killed him. Nothing else to investigate."

"Have you read the play?" Nikolai asked. "That's not what happened. That's only what it looked like on the surface. Shakespeare's story was much more complicated."

"Maybe it was, but this isn't Shakespeare here. It's simple. Tragic but simple."

Vanya pushed the newspaper with the completed crossword puzzle aside. "What did you really want to talk to me about, Nikolai?"

"About your security system."

"Why? It's all fine. We have the fence, the gate, what else is there to it?"

"Many things."

"Like what?" Vanya said.

"What do you see on your screen when a car comes to the gate?" Nikolai said.

"We see the car, of course. And we open the gate after we identify it. And only after we identify it."

"But what if somebody else is driving the car? And your real driver is dead in the snowdrift somewhere? Would you even know it?"

Vanya waved him away. "You've been watching too many spy movies. Things like that don't happen here. Plus, you're not my boss. I do things the way I do them, and everything is just fine. This conversation is over."

Avoiding further confrontation, Nikolai stepped out of the security office and started walking the perimeter of the fence. If he was going to work here for the next few weeks and protect Natalya, he needed to get a good understanding of the whole compound.

The fence was flimsy at best, and not all there. Nikolai leaned in to inspect what looked like a gap large enough for an average-size person to squeeze through. Sure enough, one post was missing, and the fence was sloppily tied together with twisted wire. One snip with metal cutters, and another entrance would appear. And this entrance would have no security cameras, no gate, and no surveillance. Nikolai heard footsteps behind him and turned around.

It was Vanya, his hands balled into fists, and his eyes glowering with anger.

"You think you're a big shot, don't you? You come from Moscow with your fancy little interpreter girl and your fancy bodyguard title, and you think you know how things are supposed to be done? I've lived here my whole life, and I've worked security since I was eighteen. In this very town. Don't you think I know better how things work here? Don't you think I understand the people and what they're after better than you do?"

"I'm not questioning your knowledge," Nikolai said. "I was just trying to help. Sometimes, it's hard to see your own problems, and I found one for you. Take a look." He pointed to the wire.

"Fine. We'll fix it. Like I need your help," Vanya said, turned around, and walked away.

Nikolai headed back to Pyotr Alekseevich's office. A blast of warm air hit him the second he opened the door to the building. He drew in a sharp breath and glanced at his watch. It was after five. Moscow was in the same time zone, so Olga must be done with work by now. She should be able to pick up the phone and talk to him. The real question was whether she would want to talk to him.

He rubbed his sore leg and dialed Olga's number. She answered on the second ring. And she sounded cheerful. Maybe, she wasn't as mad at him as she had seemed when they last talked. Or she was just happy he was away.

"I'm sorry about the other day," Nikolai said. "You're smart and competent, and I wasn't questioning that. But people can be manipulative and have their own interests in minds. I just want you to be careful. Don't accept a new job until you really know what is involved. Chief accountants have a lot of responsibilities and a lot of legal obligations. And all that can have serious consequences."

"I know, but being a chief accountant would be a great career move. I wouldn't stay long in that position, just long enough to get experience and move forward," Olga said.

"Have you talked to Denis Fedorovich lately?"

"Yes, I have. And I also talked to my current boss," Olga said.

"And what did they all say?"

"I got the offer for a promotion from my current company and the official job offer from Denis Fedorovich. So, I have choices now."

"Did you find out more about his company and that merger he mentioned?"

"Not yet. He said the merger is still in the making. But I know I like my new salary." Olga giggled.

"Please don't rush to accept his offer. I don't trust him. You'll have other opportunities. We need to be careful."

"We? It's my job, and you worry too much," Olga said. "Thanks for the flowers and the note, by the way."

Nikolai hesitated for a moment. "Are you still mad at me? Just don't do anything drastic. We really should talk. I'm sorry."

"We need to talk, I agree. But later. How's your assignment? And your new client?"

"Nothing too exciting. The town is tiny, dark and freezing cold, and the girl is spoiled. I'm sure she won't last here too long, and I'll be back in Moscow."

Olga clicked off, and Nikolai headed to Pyotr Alekseevich's office, still thinking about Olga and her job offer. She was making a mistake, and Nikolai was determined to do anything he could to convince her not to accept it. He started walking up the steps and almost ran into Natalya who was hurrying down.

"Where are you going in such a hurry?" Nikolai said.

"Bathroom. Want to come with me?" Natalya said. "I might need your protection. You never know where danger can lurk." She chuckled.

"Thanks, but I'd rather go chat with Pyotr Alekseevich. I'll see you back there."

Nikolai reached Pyotr Alekseevich's office and paused by the closed door. Pyotr Alekseevich was talking on the phone, his voice sounded agitated. Nikolai leaned in. He could not make out all the words. He heard Pyotr Alekseevich say something about the previous director, a school needing repairs, bids received from the environmental consulting companies, and the slow pipeline construction. Nothing out of the ordinary, these were the usual issues that a company director would deal with. But something in Pyotr Alekseevich's tone sounded strange: he was too emotional for a seasoned manager, too agitated. And Pyotr Alekseevich did not seem the type who would overreact. Was there something more going on that Nikolai did not know about?

Chapter Five

Nikolai stepped aside from the door and towards one of the windows. He pushed aside the brightly-colored curtain and looked out. On the outside, the glass was caked with a thick layer of snow. The last hint of twilight was already fading into the dark cold night. Days were short, just a few hours of weak light. Upper Luzinsk would not see sunshine or even real daylight until spring.

Nikolai could not imagine living here his whole life. From here, his home in Moscow felt like the tropics. He chuckled at the thought. Moscow's northern climate was hardly the tropics, but Luzinsk was extreme north, as far north as Nikolai had ever been.

"Waiting for me?" Natalya said, interrupting his thoughts. "I'm back, all safe and alive. No bad guys in the bathroom." She opened the door and walked into the office. Nikolai followed. "Let me make coffee for all of us," she said. "Pyotr Alekseevich, you like coffee, right?"

"Yes and thank you for the offer, but I make my own coffee," Pyotr Alekseevich said. "And when you taste it, you'll know why. I like it black and strong."

Nikolai's phone rang, and he stepped into the hallway. It was Anatoly, and his tone sounded serious. "Vasily Petrovich is coming by today," Anatoly said. "He wanted me to tell you how grateful he is to you. We're working on finding a new bodyguard for him, a temporary replacement while you're guarding girls in the tundra. But he really wants to work with you, once you're totally recovered."

"Sounds good to me. Any news from the investigation of the attempt on him?"

"Pretty sketchy still. Vasily Petrovich said he'd tell me more in person, but he mentioned a deal between the government and Luzinsk Oil."

"Luzinsk Oil? The company here?"

"Yes. As the lawyer for the government, he was against this deal, so he refused to sign the papers."

"What deal are we talking about?"

"He'll tell me more about it when he gets here, but you know what's interesting? That attack on him happened the day after his refusal to sign whatever it was. I don't think it was a coincidence."

"Somebody is trying to get rid of him?" Nikolai said.

"If he's replaced with a more agreeable person, the deal can go through, that's how I read this," Anatoly said. "Anything I need to know from your end?"

"There was one unusual incident that ended with a security guard getting killed, but it was over a woman, not business-related from what I can tell."

"Any details I need to know about?" Anatoly said.

"Not at the moment."

"All right. Thanks. Keep me informed."

When Nikolai walked back into the office, Pyotr Alekseevich was handing papers and brochures to Natalya, and she was putting them into her bag.

"The boss says we're done for the day," she said to Nikolai. "Computers have been slow all afternoon, so Oleg's coming to check things. And that means I can't type any translations."

"What are all these papers for?" Nikolai said.

"I need to read them tonight so I'm better prepared for the meeting tomorrow. All this technical information is pretty complicated," Natalya said.

"Thanks, Natalya. I appreciate all your efforts," Pyotr Alekseevich said. "I promise that your computer will be in a much better shape tomorrow. They tend to slow down once in a while, but Oleg knows how to fix them. They are lightning fast after he does his magic. You know where the hotel is, right? Or do you want me to send someone with you?"

"Thank you, but we'll be fine," Nikolai said. "Natalya and I can walk over there on our own."

"Sounds good. Just don't expect much. It's a small town, you know. The hotel used to be a dorm for the construction workers."

"Yes, Oleg already warned us about it," Nikolai said.

Outside, the only light came from the lit windows and industrial-style lamp posts that marked the paths between the buildings. Everything off the path looked completely dark, and Nikolai could not even tell how deep the snow was around them or how far the hotel was. He felt like he was walking into a black hole. Then, suddenly, the path stopped.

"We're home," Nikolai said, pointing to the nondescript entrance with a plain-looking sign Hotel, a bright spotlight shining on it.

"I see what he meant when he said not to expect much," Natalya said.

Nikolai pulled the heavy door open. "After you."

The reception area consisted of a desk behind which an old woman sat on a chair. Her head was covered with a scarf, and only the top button on her coat was unbuttoned despite the relative warmth of the building. On the wall next to her was a plywood board with room keys hanging on it. All keys were attached to what looked like huge wooden chess pieces. Pawns, probably. Nikolai chuckled to himself. Freud could write a paper or two about the subliminal messages these pawn-shaped key rings sent to the Soviet construction workers who used to live here.

"Are you the ones who wanted a suite?" the woman asked them. "Oleg told me when he brought your bags. Your room is on the second floor. All the way to the right. Room twelve. And you'll even have your own shower. Only five rooms in this whole hotel have their own. Most use the hallway shower. You're lucky." She stretched her arm to the board with keys, took one off, and handed it to Nikolai. "Make sure to turn in the key when you leave the hotel every morning. That way, you can't lose it, and I'll keep an eye on the key and on your room."

Nikolai and Natalya climbed the steep and narrow staircase to the second floor. They walked on the well-worn institutional-style brown carpet to the room, floorboards creaking and squeaking with each step. Room twelve was at the end of the dimly lit hallway, all the way to the right, just like the old woman told them. Nikolai put the key in the rickety lock, jiggled it a little, and opened the creaky door. The suite was more than modest, by anybody's standards. A small antechamber was equipped with a metal coat rack and a single light bulb hanging down on a thick black cord.

"Lenin's lamp," Natalya said. "How frugal."

Nikolai chuckled. He had not heard this expression for a long time, probably because he had not seen this type of lighting for a long time. The words "Lenin's lamp" used to refer to the official propaganda of Lenin's efforts to bring electricity to villages and small towns after the 1917 socialist revolution. Later, as Russian people got disillusioned with the dream of socialist heaven on earth, Lenin's lamp became a symbol of the ultimate simplicity and frugality of the new way of life that Bolsheviks brought to the people of Russia: even a simple lampshade was considered bourgeois, so the pear-shaped lamp hung free on its cord, casting harsh light on its surroundings. That was the way of life Bolsheviks advocated for the masses, reserving the finer things in life for their own use. So much for a classless society.

The antechamber had four inside doors, all open at the moment, that led to two rooms, a kitchen, and a bathroom. The furniture and the decor looked simple and minimalistic: a couch, a table, a few chairs, plain-looking wallpaper, a table lamp with a green plastic shade, thread-bare rugs, and faded curtains. Just the necessities.

"Pick your room," Nikolai said.

"I'll take this one," Natalya said and walked into the one closer to the kitchen. "It has a larger radiator. I get really cold when I sleep."

"Fine with me," Nikolai said. "Mind if I jump in the shower first?"

"Go ahead. I want to read the brochures anyway."

The hot water felt rejuvenating and refreshing after a day of traveling and being in the cold. As the hot water released the tension in Nikolai's muscles, his wounded leg immediately felt better, the last of the ache quickly disappearing. Standing under the steaming water stream, Nikolai tried to convince himself that this assignment would not be as boring as it was shaping up to be. There were definite positives. For one, he wasn't stuck in his apartment doing nothing. Two, Pyotr Alekseevich seemed like a nice man, and even Natalya was not as bad as he first thought. Being an interpreter, and a good one, was not an easy job, so she must have put a lot of effort into her studies. Maybe, her dad was too hard on her. Nikolai turned off the water, dried off, and got dressed before he stepped back into the room. He already felt better. Natalya was in the kitchen, bustling around.

"I'm making tea," she said. "Oh, some girl called. I told her you were in the shower."

"You told her what?" Nikolai grabbed his phone from the kitchen table.

"That you were in the shower."

"Did you get her name?"

"Olga, I think."

Nikolai shook his head, suppressed a wave of anger towards Natalya, and dialed Olga's number. She was not picking up, as he had expected. She was probably really mad by now, and for what looked like a good reason. More Othello and Desdemona-style jealousy and suspected affairs, just like in Vanya's crossword.

Another misunderstanding. There seemed to be a lot of that going around in Upper Luzinsk.

Last time Nikolai talked to Olga, he failed to mention that he and Natalya were sharing a suite. He thought he was doing what was better for everyone. That was a mistake. Now, Olga will not want to talk to him at all.

Frustrated, Nikolai stuck the phone into his jeans pocket and turned to Natalya. "And why are you even picking up my phone?"

"Oh, I am sorry. Did I say something wrong? Is Olga your girlfriend? I was just trying to help."

"Please don't help anymore," Nikolai said. "Why did you do that? Do you know what she will think now? How am I going to explain you to her?" A new wave of anger came over him. Not only was he stuck with Natalya in this awful little town on a pointless assignment, now she was ruining what was left of his personal life, too. He should have taken Anatoly's offer to teach at the academy. That would have been of more use to everyone, no doubt.

"Don't worry so much," Natalya said. "She'll forgive you."

"Like you would know. Just don't touch my phone ever again," Nikolai said, trying to regain composure.

"Agreed. I'm sorry. But let me make it up to you. You just have a seat and relax, and I'll make some tea. It's jasmine and chamomile, soothes the soul and calms the nerves. You do drink tea, I hope?"

"I drink tea, sure." Nikolai grabbed a chair, flipped it around and sat down, reminding himself that whether he liked it or not, Natalya was still his client, so getting to know her better was a part of his job.

Natalya turned on the electric stove, poured some tap water into the small kettle, and put two cups and a small ceramic teapot on the counter.

"Another benefit of having the suite," she said. "Comes with all the essentials." She scooped out loose tea from a small tin. "Why don't you tell me how you became a bodyguard while the tea is brewing. Was it your childhood dream?" She chuckled. "Other boys wanted to fly into space or discover cures for diseases, and you wanted to guard people?"

"Yes, that's exactly how it was. And in my next life, I hope to be reincarnated as a German shepherd."

"Come on, don't get upset. I was just joking, trying to lift your mood, you know. But really, how did you become a bodyguard?"

"I don't think you really want to know," Nikolai said.

"I do, honestly. I'm sorry if I haven't been the best person to work with, but I'll try to make your job easier." Natalya poured the tea into cups and handed one cup to Nikolai. "Here, you need to relax."

Nikolai took a sip. The tea was hot and strong, with an unusual aftertaste that Nikolai could not identify, minty and earthy. "Good tea."

"My secret recipe." Natalya giggled. "Come on, tell me, how did you get into this job?"

"It just happened."

Natalya gave him a pouty look, got up and walked into her room. Another upset woman, Nikolai thought. Going for the record of the highest number of women I manage to offend in one day. So far so good. While Nikolai contemplated apologizing to Natalya, her door opened again, and she came out with a box of chocolate candy.

"Peace?" she said and placed the box on the table in front of Nikolai. "Have some."

"Thanks. But why don't you talk about yourself first." Nikolai rubbed his leg, took one piece, and put it into his mouth. Natalya wasn't his favorite person at the moment, but he reminded himself that he needed to make an effort to get to know her better so they could develop some trust and be able to discuss their plans for each day and their strategy for dealing with potential threats, foreseen and unforeseen. That was a part of his job, so he needed to get over the situation with Olga and focus on the job. Nikolai smiled and said, "Thanks for the chocolate. So, tell me, how did you become an interpreter?"

"Not much to tell. I've always been independent, so this kind of work suits me well. I never wanted to work in a big office, and I did not want to have the same boss or the same colleagues for too long."

"Why not?"

"I don't want to get attached to people too much. I like my freedom. And interpreting is perfect: I get to learn about a lot of different areas, meet different people, and, in the case of this job especially, makes some decent money."

"I thought this was your first job," Nikolai said.

"My first real job, away from home. I had short-term assignments before, mostly in Moscow. Anyway, your turn. You must be really brave and fearless to be a bodyguard. Are you?"

"I don't know about fearless. I've learned to tell the difference between fear and danger and found ways to deal with both."

"Most people don't like dealing with either."

"Maybe not. But I didn't see any other choices for myself. We don't like to admit it, but a lot of important events in our lives are shaped by circumstances, and that was the case for me, too."

"Circumstances? How so?" Natalya said.

"I come from a military family and since I was a kid, I always imagined myself a warrior, invincible and brave. As I grew up, I became more realistic but no less idealistic about the military career. But after I graduated from the military academy, all the military cuts started, and there were no real jobs for recent graduates, at least not the ones I trained for. I was stuck in an office shuffling papers and waiting for the final discharge. Then, a friend of mine asked me to be present at a business deal, just in case something went wrong. You never know how these so-called business deals can turn out. I came along and met his boss. The brother of the boss owned the bodyguard agency. One thing led to another, and now I'm here."

"So, do they teach you how to fight and use weapons?"

"I already knew how to do that. My military academy, remember?"

"Are you always armed?" Natalya said.

"With knowledge and skills," Nikolai said. "And a sharp wit."

"No really, where do you keep your weapons?"

"The weapons are called concealed for a reason. You don't need to worry about things like that. Your job here is stressful enough. All that interpreting must be tiresome."

"It's stressful sometimes, especially if people I'm interpreting for get impatient or start interrupting each other. Sometimes, they get so worked up about an issue, they start talking faster and faster, forgetting that I'm there struggling to keep up with the conversation. At other times, people don't take any time to formulate their thoughts. They just say the first thing that comes to their mind, in whatever way it comes, and change sentence structure as they go. When it comes out awkward in the other language or people don't understand them, they think it's the interpreter's lack of skills. But it's not always the case."

"Pyotr Aleksecvich seems quite impressed with your interpreting. How did you get so good at it?"

"Like anyone who is good at anything. Lots of studying and lots of practice. My college trained us well for interpreting. Of course, some of the terms here are new to me: casing, piping, drill bits, and other oil field terms can be hard to remember right away, but Pyotr Alekseevich seems to know these words in English, and I'm learning fast."

"Have you always been a good student?" Nikolai said.

"Sure. I'm ambitious, you know, despite what my dad says."

Nikolai nodded, took the last sip of his tea, and felt the warmth spread all over his body. He was seeing a very different side of Natalya: not the spoiled rich and immature girl but an educated, intelligent, and hard-working young woman. Was all that surface immaturity just her way to interact with her dad because he did not take her seriously? Maybe, the real reason she was here was to prove something to her dad or just to get away from his watchful eyes. Hence, Nikolai's job.

"Aren't you a little bored here?" Nikolai asked. "It's not exactly a bustling place."

"I'll find a way to entertain myself, don't worry," Natalya said and smiled coyly.

"I have no doubt about that." He suppressed a yawn. Natalya still seemed lively, perky, and very much awake. But it was late, and Nikolai was tired. More tired than he would want to admit.

70

"More tea?" Natalya asked. "It's good for you." She poured another cup for Nikolai. He took it and was about to take a sip when he noticed that Natalya's cup was still full.

Chapter Six

Nikolai took his cup and got up. "Thanks for the tea, Natalya, but I'd better go to bed. You should, too. It was a long day, and we both need some rest."

Nikolai said goodnight, walked into his room, put the cup on the bedside table, lay on top of his bed, all his clothes still on and his Makarov still in the shoulder holster, and closed his eyes. He thought about doing the stretching exercises for his leg that the doctor taught him but felt too tired. He decided to rest for a few moments. What felt like minutes later, he heard loud music. It was making Nikolai's head throb. The melody sounded familiar, but he couldn't figure out where it was coming from or why it was so loud. He opened his eyes and saw his phone. Fighting off the grip of sleep, Nikolai stretched his arm towards his phone on the nightstand and quieted the alarm. He felt a movement next to him in bed and jumped up. Instinctively, he checked his holster. His pistol was still there.

"Natalya? What are you doing here? Get out of my bed," he said, averting his eyes from the little lacy thing she was wearing. "And get dressed." He threw a blanket over her.

She smiled sweetly but did not move. "I just thought you would want some company, with Olga not here and mad at you."

"Olga is not mad at me. And that's none of your business anyway."

"I was just trying to help," Natalya said.

"I thought we had already agreed that you will not be trying to help," Nikolai said.

"You're quite a sleeper," Natalya said. "Nothing could wake you up."

"I can wake up when I need to. Enough of these games. And enough of your help, really." He stepped out of the room and into the kitchen. "Get dressed," he called out to Natalya.

He was obviously mistaken about Natalya. Again. After their conversation the night before, Nikolai had thought she could behave like an adult, and that her promise not to make this job difficult for him was honest and sincere. He no longer thought that. Her interpreting skills aside, she was childish, self-centered, and immature. The only thing he believed now is that she would be looking for a way, any way, to entertain herself, just like she told him.

Nikolai picked up his phone and dialed Olga's number. No response. He clicked off. No point leaving a message.

"Olga's not there again? It's dangerous to leave women alone, you know." Dressed in tight jeans and an oversized navy-blue sweater, Natalya walked into the kitchen.

"You need to get to the office," Nikolai said. "Let's go."

More snow fell overnight, covering the roofs, the parked cars, obscuring the paths, and making the snowplows inside and outside the compound work even harder to make the roads usable. Nikolai and Natalya had to find the path in all the blowing snow and newly formed ice. Twice, Nikolai had to pull Natalya out of the deep snow when she stepped off the path. The wind that picked up in the early morning hadn't died down. Despite the thick parka, the hat, and the scarf, the snow blew into Nikolai's collar, freezing his neck. Natalya was shivering. Finally, the familiar entrance with a spotlight on either side came into view.

"Can't wait to get inside," Natalya said.

"My sentiments exactly," Nikolai said.

They came up to the entrance at the same time as Pyotr Alekseevich did. He held the door open for them. "I'm glad you're here early," he said to Natalya. "I'll need your help talking to the Canadians. We have to get a lot done before the Board meeting next week."

"Sure," Natalya said. "How are the computers?"

"Great," Pyotr Alekseevich said. "Oleg fixed everything, so you'll be able to use your computer again when we get back."

"I'm coming with you to the meeting," Nikolai said. "You don't object, Pyotr Alekseevich, do you?"

"Fine with me," Pyotr Alekseevich said and the three of them headed up the stairs.

"You can sit there, Nikolai." Pyotr Alekseevich pointed to an armchair in the corner of the small conference room. Next to it, a small couch was piled high with heavy coats and hats. Nikolai took his coat off, tucked his cap inside the sleeve, added his coat to the pile, and looked around.

A table with eight chairs was in the middle of the room, with maps of the oil field and various other papers scattered around. Three Canadian men, all dressed in jeans, big boots, and fleece jackets over their shirts sat on the right side of the table. Across from them sat two Russian men, dressed in dark pants and thick sweaters. Each group was quietly talking among themselves. Nikolai poured himself a cup of coffee, grabbed a local newspaper off a side table, and settled in the chair.

"What we need to discuss today," Pyotr Alekseevich addressed the group in Russian, and Natalya repeated his words in English, speaking clearly and confidently, "is the proposed schedule for repayment of the old taxes. This is our last chance to show the government that we are serious about keeping this company alive. The other pressing issues are the evaluation of bids from two environmental consulting companies and replacing sections of the old pipeline."

Nikolai kept listening to the conversation while leafing through the newspaper. Unpaid taxes was serious business. Apparently, the previous director did not think that paying taxes was necessary, and that's what almost closed down the company. No wonder Pyotr Alekseevich was revered by everyone so much: it sounded like it was his hard work and his good reputation that convinced the regional authorities to appeal to the central government to keep the company alive and allow Pyotr Alekseevich and his Board members to come up with a schedule for repayment of the old taxes. The previous director was now under investigation for tax evasion, and big money was at stake for many people.

About half-an-hour into the meeting, Nikolai's phone buzzed quietly in his pocket. He glanced at the number and stepped into the hallway.

"Any news?" Anatoly said.

"Not much." Nikolai told Anatoly what he had learned about the unpaid taxes, the previous director, and the upcoming Board meeting.

"How's Natalya? Nothing dangerous around there, I take it?"

"She's the dangerous one." Nikolai chuckled. "I don't envy her dad. Or any of her boyfriends. But anyway, in the interests of due diligence, can you check the backgrounds of a few characters for me? I don't think any of them have any ties to Natalya or any reasons to want to harm her, but I want to make sure."

"Of course."

Nikolai gave Anatoly the names of the people who were coming to the Board meeting from Moscow and walked back into the conference room. The meeting was breaking up. The Canadians were heading out, and Pyotr Alekseevich was busy talking to the Russian group.

Natalya came up to Nikolai. "So how's your girlfriend?" she said. "You couldn't even wait until the meeting was over to talk to her, could you?"

Nikolai was about to tell Natalya that it was not Olga he was talking to but changed his mind.

"No, I couldn't," he said deciding that playing along with Natalya and letting her believe he was focused on Olga would be a good idea. Misdirection could come in handy. Natalya was manipulative and, like all manipulative people, looked for vulnerabilities in others so she could use them to her advantage. Nikolai did not yet understand what advantage she was after, but leading her to believe that he was more concerned about the situation with Olga than he actually was could prevent Natalya from searching for other vulnerabilities in Nikolai. And it might keep Natalya out of his bed, an added bonus.

Natalya smiled coyly. "Must be true love. I hope she feels the same."

"I hope she does. But Moscow can be exciting, you know," Nikolai said. "Of course, excitement is about people, not places. Even small towns have plenty of exciting people."

"Just don't think I'm interested in you," Natalya said. "Now that I know you better, I see why Olga is losing interest in you and looking for excitement elsewhere."

"And why is that?" Nikolai asked.

"You're too safe, too reliable, too predictable. No sense of adventure, no spontaneity. And what girl wants that? We like excitement. Like you said, excitement is about people."

"I see. I'll have to think about it." Something seemed strange about Natalya. He could not figure out why she kept bringing up Olga. Jealousy? But Natalya did not seem interested in Nikolai, and she probably knew she was too young for him. Her comments seemed purposeful, but Nikolai did not know what that purpose was. He had always thought he could read people pretty well, but this wasn't the case with Natalya. At least not yet.

Pyotr Alekseevich came up to them. "Thank you again, Natalya. With a different interpreter, we would be here for another hour or more. You did a great job."

"Would you like me to finish those written translations now?" Natalya asked.

"Yes, please," Pyotr Alekseevich said. "On second thought, no. The translations can wait. Why don't you come with me to look at the pipeline progress. There's nothing there to translate, but it will be a nice break from the office. You'll get to go outside the compound and see the real north. And the real oil field."

Outside, Pyotr Alekseevich led them to a company-owned Land Rover parked in front of the building. He sat down in the driver's seat.

"Do you often drive yourself?" Nikolai asked Pyotr Alekseevich.

"Most of the time. I like driving, especially in this rugged open space."

Pyotr Alekseevich steered the Land Rover out of the gates, waved to Vanya through the window, and headed up the same main thoroughfare that connected the airport to Luzinsk. They headed away from the airport, further north.

"This might be your last chance to see the oil field since we're getting to the end of the driving season," Pyotr Alekseevich said.

"What do you mean?" Natalya said.

"These are not permanent roads," Pyotr Alekseevich said. "You can't build a permanent road here. It's too swampy, so all these roads out to the oil fields are made out of tightly packed snow and can be used only in the winter. In the summer, the snow and the roads melt away, so we have to plan all construction accordingly. It's impossible to transport materials by land vehicles once the snow starts melting. The whole area turns into one giant mosquito-infested swamp. Luckily, the winters are long."

"But what supports the oil derricks in the summer?" Nikolai asked. "How do they not sink into the swamps?"

"We put them on large concrete pads that distribute the weight evenly and allow the derricks to remain in place. But when something needs repairs in the summer, it's a real challenge to get to these areas. Most of the time, we have to use helicopters. And that's expensive. Really expensive."

The Land Rover passed a plain-looking weathered sign on the side of the road. For a moment, Nikolai wondered about the need for a traffic sign in this emptiness. As they came closer, he glanced at it. It said simply, *The Arctic Circle*.

"We're almost at the main oil field," Pyotr Alekseevich said as the road curved around a large snowdrift, and the Land Rover entered a vast open space. The thin bright line on the horizon was fading, and the only light came from the bright glow of the large full moon on the cloudless sky. The snow-covered expanse around them shimmered in the light. The land looked pristine and isolated.

"It's like a different universe," Natalya said.

"It is a different universe," Pyotr Alekseevich said. "I like coming out here. It's truly a no man's land. Civilization is barely reaching here. No cell towers and no communications here besides two-way radios. But keep your eyes open."

He slowed down and steered the Land Rover around a large hill. As soon as they cleared the corner, bright orange flares of burning oil and black iron lattice towers of oil derricks came into view, an industrial intrusion into the arctic wilderness. Nikolai could see workers, dressed in parkas and wearing protective helmets, move around the derricks.

Pyotr Alekseevich kept driving until the industrial structures disappeared from view. He pulled over next to a concrete pad largely obscured by a thick layer of snow, turned off the engine but left the high beams on.

"Ready to see the pipeline?" he asked.

"Sure," Natalya said and came out of the car. Nikolai followed.

A pipeline of about half a meter in diameter came out of the ground and zigzagged through the white snow-covered hills, its weight supported by heavy metal poles on both sides. The poles were placed every few meters along the pipeline.

"Our pride and joy," Pyotr Alekseevich said. "It's the new pipeline. No more leaks or spills into the rivers and onto the land."

"Were there leaks before?" Nikolai asked.

Pyotr Alekseevich nodded. "Major ones, and nobody cared. Environmental protection laws are pretty lax, and the previous management did not care about pollution. Things got really bad. You could throw a lit match into the river, and it would catch on fire."

"The whole river?" Natalya asked.

"The spilled oil created a film on the surface, and that's what burned, but it looked like the whole river was on fire. It was hell on earth, but Moscow managers did not care much. As long as the profit was there, they considered it a successful operation. It's different for me. I grew up here, I know and love this land. I go fishing in the summer, skiing in the winter. This is my home, and I want to keep it clean." Pyotr Alekseevich paused and drew in a long breath. "We still have a few more smaller pipes to replace that are getting corroded, but this one was the worst."

"Where does this pipeline go?" Natalya asked.

"From the oil field to the terminal in Upper Luzinsk and then on to the refineries down south." Pyotr Alekseevich took one more look at the pipeline.

"Shall we?" He motioned to the car.

"That's all you needed to do here?" Natalya asked. "Look at the pipeline?"

"I just needed a break from the office. Coming out here helps clear my mind and focus on what's important. But we should get back. I need to read over the bids again for the new environmental consulting company. Our environmental impact numbers should be much better this year, thanks to this pipeline."

Chapter Seven

With a few hours left in the workday, Natalya and Pyotr Alekseevich headed back to the office, and Nikolai went to talk to Vanya about the latest security improvements. Nikolai was getting used to the short distances and tall snowdrifts. There was a strange sense of freedom in not having to wait for cars, buses, or spend any time in transit. He could get anywhere he needed in a matter of minutes, and the street lights pointed his way in the permanent semi darkness of the arctic winter. An added benefit was that his leg was feeling better and better, probably partially due to all the walking he was doing. Nikolai was sure he would remember this assignment and this town for a long time. It was so different from anything he had experienced or could have even imagined.

When the two young guards in the security office saw Nikolai, they jumped up from their lunch of salami sandwiches and pickles and tried to look busy. They were obviously relieved when Nikolai made no comments about their activities.

"Looking for Vanya?" one of the young guards asked. "He's in there." The guard pointed to the door that led from the security office to the garage.

The garage was small, with the space for two cars, but only one car was kept there, Pyotr Alekseevich's BMW. The rest of the space was taken by workshop tables, benches, and various tools. Vanya liked tinkering with things, especially rare and expensive things, so he enjoyed cleaning and polishing the BMW himself, never hiring anyone else to do it.

When Nikolai walked in, Vanya sat at the desk, fussing with wires, cable boxes, and light bulbs spread out in front of him.

"Busy?" Nikolai said.

"Just working on security lights. A couple of connections were malfunctioning, so I need to solder them."

"I see."

In the corner, a small TV was broadcasting a hockey game.

"Who's winning?" Nikolai asked.

"Not my team, so nobody. Nothing but disappointment this whole game." Vanya adjusted the desk lamp and leaned in closer to his project. "Just turn the stupid thing off."

Nikolai walked over to the TV, clicked it off, and leaned against the wall to admire Pyotr Alekseevich's silver BMW SUV parked in its usual place. The car was a beauty, with leather seats and a nice trim. And Vanya kept it clean and in top shape.

"Any news on our killer husband?" Nikolai asked, his eyes still on the BMW.

"Not yet."

Something on the door of the car caught his attention. Was it dirt? Nikolai came closer. It was a small scratch mark, and it looked fresh.

"Did you see this thing?" he asked Vanya.

"What thing? What are you finding now, Sherlock?" Vanya asked without looking up.

"Come see for yourself."

Vanya set his tools down, got up, and walked over to Nikolai.

"See?" Nikolai pointed to the scratch mark.

"Didn't notice it before. What a shame." Vanya leaned in and inspected the mark closer, tracing the length of the line with his finger. "But it's not deep. I'm pretty sure I can polish it away. No major harm done, luckily."

"Not yet," Nikolai said.

"What's that supposed to mean?" Vanya said.

"When was the last time Pyotr Alekseevich used the car?"

"Yesterday morning. Why?"

"Did you clean it after that?"

"In this weather? Of course. I clean it after each trip."

"And you did not notice the scratch?"

"I guess I did not. What are you implying?"

"I know why you did not see it," Nikolai said.

"All right. Enlighten me. Why?" Hands on his hips, his gaze intense and defiant, Vanya looked straight at Nikolai.

"Because it wasn't there when you cleaned it. It's new. And I bet it's related to this thing." Nikolai pointed to a large flower basket on the chair by the door.

"What? To the flowers? You're not making any sense. I need to take this basket to the conference room. Just didn't get a chance to do it yet."

"Did you see who brought it?" Nikolai said.

"No. It was delivered earlier today, while I was out."

"That figures."

"What figures? How? Are you saying that whoever delivered the basket scratched the car?" Vanya glared at Nikolai.

"Not exactly."

"I wasn't here," Vanya said, his tone changing from defiant to defensive. "But it's addressed to Pyotr Alekseevich. That's all I need to know."

Nikolai picked up the basket, plucked out the note, read it, and nodded.

"Interesting greeting." He handed Vanya the note. "Take a look."

There was only one typed line on the note, no signature, and no return address.

Congratulations on the sale of the company. Safe travels!

"He's selling the company?" Vanya said. "I didn't know that." He looked up at Nikolai, his expression registering a surprise realization. "He isn't selling, is he?"

"No. And I can't tell if this note is a threat or a warning. But it makes me want to inspect the car. Hand me the car keys, please."

This time, Vanya did not ask any questions. He simply walked to his desk, reached into a drawer, took the keys out, and handed them to Nikolai.

Using the key instead of the clicker, Nikolai unlocked the scratched door and opened it just a crack. With his ID card, he slowly traced a line all along the opening. Sure enough, the ID card snagged a thin wire.

"You don't have a telescopic pole with mirror, do you?" he asked Vanya.

"What's that?"

"A device to search for objects mounted to the undercarriage."

"What kind of objects are we talking about?" Vanya's voice sounded nervous.

"I don't know yet, and that's exactly what I need the telescopic pole for."

"I don't have one, and you are really scaring me now. Are we talking a bomb under the car or something?"

"Anything is possible, but let's not jump to conclusions yet," Nikolai said. "Do you have a regular mirror and a rag? And a flashlight?"

"Sure, sure. Just give me a second." Vanya bustled about the garage and brought a large paper bag filled with rags, a flashlight and two hand-held mirrors of different sizes.

Nikolai spread one of the wider and thicker rags on the floor next to the passenger side of the car, put the larger of the two mirrors on top of it, facing up, and slowly slid the rag under the car.

"Here, hold the flashlight and shine it at an angle," he said to Vanya. "Like this. That way, the reflection doesn't blind me, and we can both see what's under the body of the car."

Vanya did what Nikolai asked him to and stared at the car. Nikolai bent down and carefully slid the mirror down the length of the car by gently pulling on the rag. Soon, he saw what he was looking for. The wire from the door led to a small rectangular-shaped object mounted under the car. That object was not a part of the car.

"Vanya, see it? This box under the car? Whoever put it in must have been in a hurry and scratched the car."

"A box under the car? Why?" Vanya said. "What is it?"

"Let me check."

"Is it a listening device? Or a bomb?" Vanya exclaimed and stepped away. "Be careful, please. Should I call someone?"

"Hold on a second," Nikolai said.

He took the flashlight and peered under the car. The last thing he and Vanya needed was to have an explosion right here, with both of them in the garage. For a moment, he contemplated asking Vanya if there was a bomb squad in the area, but as he inspected the device more, he changed his mind. Nikolai took his Swiss army knife out of his pocket, dropped to his knees, stretched his right hand under the car, and snipped the wire.

Vanya gasped. "What are you doing? It'll blow up!" He rushed to the door.

Nikolai pulled off the rectangular object, its shiny wrapper embossed with the words *Happy New Year!*

"It's a firecracker! A stupid firecracker," he said.

"So, it's not dangerous?" Vanya asked from the door, his expression still worried.

"It's not dangerous," he said to Vanya. "But if Pyotr Alekseevich fully opened the door, like everyone does, the wire would have pulled the ring out and there would have been a lot of noise and smoke. It wouldn't have killed him, but it would have really scared him."

"Who do you think did it?" Vanya said. "I can't imagine who would be capable of doing this or how they got in here."

"I'm new to this town, so I don't have too many theories," Nikolai said. "Let's think. You said you weren't here when that basket was delivered, but do you know who was here?"

"One of the security guys. I can probably check to find out who it was."

"What's your protocol for deliveries?" Nikolai asked.

"Protocol? We have none. Just receive whatever is brought in here and take it to whomever it's for. I told you, Nikolai, we've never had to deal with anything dangerous. It's a small town, and things are usually quiet here."

"Not anymore. Somebody is sending serious warnings to Pyotr Alekseevich, and they are not going to stop," Nikolai said. "You have to tell me everything you know. Have there been attempts on Pyotr Alekseevich's life before?"

"No, not real attempts."

"Care to explain?"

"A few months ago, a couple of characters came to me," Vanya said reluctantly. "They offered me a lot of money to kill Pyotr Alekseevich. That was just before he took over the company."

"So much for a small quiet town, no?"

"It was an isolated incident," Vanya said. "A fluke."

"They asked you, the company's security director, to murder him? And you call that a fluke?"

"I wasn't the security director then, and Pyotr Alekseevich was still the mayor."

"And that meant it was okay for you to kill him? I don't get your point."

"Of course not! Don't even say things like that! I just mean that I worked for the city hall, as a security guard, one of the three guards who worked there, so that's how I knew Pyotr Alekseevich."

"And then what?" Nikolai asked.

"I told Pyotr Alekseevich about it, and he appointed me head of security after he took over the company."

"Who were these people?" Nikolai asked.

"I have no idea. I had never seen them before, or after. They disappeared right after that conversation, and our investigation, with the local police, showed nothing. And nothing had happened since. It was deemed an empty threat."

"An empty threat? I'm not so sure. So, why didn't you think I would want to know about it?"

"I thought it was all in the past, that with this new compound and the new security system, things were under control. Everything has been quiet," Vanya said. "Until now."

"Why didn't you tell me about it earlier?"

"I didn't think it was any of your business, that's one reason."

"What's another reason?"

Vanya hesitated. "Look, I'm supposed to be in charge here. I'm supposed to know what's going on and be able to control it. I'm older than you and I have lived here my whole life. I'm the security expert of Upper Luzinsk, right? Then you show up, a fancy young Moscow guy, first time here and you know more than I do. I feel like a useless old fool. You could do it all on your own."

"You must be kidding," Nikolai said. "Do it all on my own? I can hardly find my way around the compound, let alone this whole town. There's no way I could do anything here without you. I don't know the people, they don't know me. Nobody would even talk to me without you. You know much more about Upper Luzinsk and the company."

"Maybe so," Vanya said. "But this?" He pointed to the car. "The telescopic pole thing, the ID card, the stretched wire. I had no clue."

"We have different work experiences, and I have had to deal with certain types of threats more. As you said yourself, life in Moscow is different than here."

"Right. Here it's just ice and snow. At least it used to be."

"But things are changing here, too," Nikolai said. "There's much more to Upper Luzinsk than ice and snow. The oil field has tremendous wealth and can attract all kinds of people, with a variety of motives. In Moscow, I've seen what money can do to people, and now I see that this small town is no different. There's a lot of wealth in your oil field and a lot of money to be made. Division of wealth can get ugly."

"I never thought it could get that bad here, real death threats and all. Right in my hometown," Vanya said.

"That's how I felt about Moscow, my hometown. If somebody would have told me some years ago that killers tried to shoot people in the middle of the day, right on a quiet street where I grew up, I would have never believed it. Now, I've experienced it myself."

"Are you serious? Did you get shot?"

"I wasn't the target, my client was. He's okay, and my leg is healing. Life is different now. In Moscow and here."

Vanya looked at Nikolai for a long moment, then nodded. "I'm glad you're okay. And thank you, Nikolai. I didn't think of things that way. It makes sense. We can learn from each other, right?"

"Of course. That's the only way to live and work."

"You're a good man, Nikolai," Vanya said. "So, what else can I tell you about this town? What would help?"

"I wish I could stay and help, but I have an obligation to Natalya, her dad, and my company to keep her safe. That's my only goal right now, and I don't feel that what's happening here is making it safe for her. There is no need for her to stay. Can you please let Pyotr Alekseevich know?"

"She's not in danger. Why don't you stay. I'm beginning to enjoy your company, you know," Vanya said. "And we could really use your help here."

"If something happens to her, it will be on my conscience, " Nikolai said. "The situation is not safe for my client. Can you please prepare a car for Natalya and me? Preferably the one without explosives. We're taking the first flight out of here."

"All right. I'll call Oleg and send the car to the hotel for you," Vanya said.

Back at the hotel suite, Nikolai quickly packed Natalya's suitcases, threw all his stuff into his duffel bag, and headed back downstairs.

Oleg's Lada was idling by the hotel entrance. Oleg stepped out of the car and opened the trunk.

"Leaving already?" Oleg said. "I thought you were going to stay longer."

"Our circumstances have changed," Nikolai said. "Pyotr Alekseevich's office, please."

Nikolai was not looking forward to what he knew would be an unpleasant scene with Natalya, but he had no choice. When he came into the office, Natalya was working on the computer. Pyotr Alekseevich left for the oil field in the morning and had not returned yet.

"We have to go back to Moscow," Nikolai said. "Right now."

"What kind of a crazy idea is that?" Natalya stopped typing and looked up at Nikolai.

"Not crazy at all. Knowing what I know now, it would be criminal for me to keep you here, and a violation of my company's contract with your father. The situation is getting dangerous and could potentially become life-threatening for anyone who works as closely with Pyotr Alekseevich as you do."

She huffed. "But what about Pyotr Alekseevich? Isn't his life in danger, too, then?"

"It may be, but it's not my job to protect him or anyone else. Just you. Vanya knows what is going on, and he will do what he needs to do to protect Pyotr Alekseevich and the others. It's not up to me. It is up to everyone else to decide what they need to do."

"Ok. Then I decide that I need to stay." She turned back to her computer.

"It's not your decision to make. My job is to protect you, so I have to make this decision for you. And my decision is to leave. Right now."

"And what if I don't want to leave? What are you going to do, kidnap me?"

"If I have to, I will. I could also call security and make the situation pretty embarrassing for you."

"Fine. But you will have to explain this to my dad,"
Natalya said. "And I guarantee that he will not be happy."
Reluctantly, she got up from the computer and walked
towards the door.

"That's his right," Nikolai said. "Let's go. The car is
waiting." He opened the office door for Natalya, and she
stepped out into the hallway.

"But what about my stuff?" she said as they walked
down the steps.

"It's packed and in the car."

"You went through my stuff?"

"Nothing there I hadn't seen before."

"But that was my personal stuff!" Natalya said,
pausing in front of the door that led outside.

"It still is." Nikolai held the door open for her and
walked her to Oleg's Lada.

"I didn't take anything, and I didn't particularly enjoy
packing it all, but I had no choice. We have to leave. Now.
Get in, please." Nikolai opened the car door for Natalya.
Reluctantly, she climbed in. At the gate, just as they were
about to leave the compound, Oleg slowed down. Vanya was
running up to the car, waving and shouting for them to wait.

"What is it?" Nikolai lowered his window. "We're
leaving."

"It's Pyotr Alekseevich." Vanya was out of breath. So
much for fit and strong security guys. "He just got back and
he needs to talk to you. Right now. Please. It sounds
important."

"All right, but it'd better be quick," Nikolai said.

Oleg turned his Lada around and drove back to the
office building.

"Please keep Natalya company while I'm gone,"
Nikolai said to Oleg and walked inside the building.

Pyotr Alekseevich motioned to the chair across from him. "Thank you for coming back, Nikolai. Please sit down." Pyotr Alekseevich's expression was serious, his face looked more lined and more tired than usual.

"I only have a few minutes," Nikolai said. "Natalya and I need to leave. What did you want to talk to me about?"

"I need your help. I understand that you know as much as Vanya about security and the situation here. Maybe more. Things are getting serious, and I don't think that Vanya and my guys can handle it all. I need somebody better trained and more professional." Pyotr Alekseevich paused and looked straight at Nikolai.

"I want to hire you as my bodyguard, just until the Board meeting is done and everything is signed. This company and this town are important to me." Pyotr Alekseevich looked straight at Nikolai.

"I am sorry but I can't do it. I'm already working for Natalya, and I can only have one client at a time. It's in my contract." Nikolai got up. "I wish I could help you more."

When Oleg's Lada finally left the compound, with Natalya pouting and Oleg pretending not to notice and making attempts at small talk, Nikolai felt a sense of relief. This had been a strange assignment and a strange client, and he looked forward to getting rid of Natalya, leaving this desolate town the affairs of which he did not quite understand, and getting back to the familiar environment of the big city. His leg was mainly healed, and he was ready for a real assignment, working with Vasily Petrovich again. And it was time to talk to Olga instead of hiding from her and their problems behind his job and his clients. She deserved better than being strung along just because Nikolai could not admit certain things to her or could not deal with the changes in their relationship and in each of their own lives and careers.

The car turned the corner, leaving Upper Luzinsk behind, and entered the main road leading to the airport. Nikolai's phone rang. It was Anatoly, and he had a change of plans in mind. Nikolai listened attentively.

"Any questions?" Anatoly said when he finished his explanation.

"No, no questions." Nikolai clicked off and addressed Oleg. "Please turn back to the compound. We are not going to the airport."

"What's going on?" Natalya said. "We're staying? My life is no longer in danger or you no longer care?"

"Neither. You will have a new bodyguard tomorrow, and I will be working for Pyotr Alekseevich. So you will be protected, don't worry."

"I hope my new bodyguard is as cute as you are," Natalya said and turned to the window. "And single."

When they returned to the compound, Natalya asked Oleg to take her to the hotel before going back to the office. Nikolai headed straight to Pyotr Alekseevich's building.

Pyotr Alekseevich was not alone in the office. A slender woman, her long dark hair in a ponytail, sat in a chair usually occupied by Natalya. They were talking in hushed tones.

When Pyotr Alekseevich saw Nikolai, he stood up to shake his hand. "Thank you for staying. Nikolai, this is Svetlana."

The woman smiled. "You can blame me for your return. I convinced Pyotr that he needed to start taking all these threats more seriously. I've been very worried."

"Nikolai," Pyotr Alekseevich said, "Svetlana is my wife. Ex-wife, to be exact, but we've been working to change that." He smiled at Svetlana, then turned back to Nikolai. "I know you and Anatoly work closely together, and I appreciate that you agreed to help us."

"I have to do what my boss tells me. It's a job."

"I'll let you two talk," Svetlana said. "Nice meeting you, Nikolai. I'll see you next week, Pyotr." She looked at her watch. "I have to get to the airport, and the driver is waiting."

She left.

"Your boss runs quite an agency," Pyotr Alekseevich said. "I must say I misunderstood what bodyguards do. Like most people, I thought it was all about guns and muscles. I didn't realize that you have to do a lot of investigations."

"Yes. This job is as much about detective work and psychology as it is about guns and muscles, probably more so. Like Anatoly likes to say, we are not paid to take a flying bullet in the head but use our head to keep that bullet from flying."

Pyotr Alekseevich nodded. "I understand it now, after discussing things with Anatoly at length, and that's exactly what I need. I hope you can help us over the days of the Board meeting. I'm worried that other Board members may be also targeted. The tax repayment plan that the government is offering needs to be signed by me and the two Board members from our company. The condition of the plan is that if one of us is not willing or not able to sign by the last day of the Board meeting, the whole deal is off, and the company has to be sold."

"I see," Nikolai said. "I apologize for being so blunt, but I have to ask you about Svetlana. Anyone close to my client is my business, and she is definitely close to you. And that's the first time I met her, so I need to know a little more."

"I understand," Pyotr Alekseevich said.

"How long ago did you get a divorce?"

"It's been fifteen years since the divorce, and we were only married for five years."

"What was the reason for the divorce? Any financial problems between the two of you?"

"No, no financial problems." Pyotr Alekseevich chuckled. "At least, nothing like people have now. Like most people fifteen years ago, we were both employed but pretty poor, at least by today's standards. I made some mistakes early in our marriage, youthful indiscretions sorts of things that I still regret. Mainly, I wasn't ready to be a dad then, and that's what started all the problems. Svetlana is a wonderful woman, but I wasn't so wonderful to her. We've been talking more lately, and we've been seeing each other more, too."

"Does she live here?"

"No, she lives in Moscow, but she visits quite often. She has a few close friends here, and lately she's been coming more often. We're working on getting back together."

"You said you weren't ready to be a dad then. Did she want kids?"

"She certainly did." Pyotr Alekseevich said. For a moment, he hesitated, looked away, then back at Nikolai. "This is hard for me to share with you, but I realize I need to. Svetlana and I had a son. He was about four when I left. I haven't seen him since the divorce."

"You haven't seen him in fifteen years?"

"That's right."

"Why not?"

"Svetlana was so upset at first that she did not want to have anything to do with me. Then, we lost touch for a few years. For quite a few years. It was only in the last twelve months or so that we started talking again. Gradually, we've been getting closer. A few weeks ago, she told me that she thinks it's time for me and our son to get re-introduced to each other. I can't tell you how happy I was to hear it. Happy and a little nervous, of course. I just can't wait to meet him."

"So, he's about nineteen or twenty now?"

"He must be," Pyotr Alekseevich said. "I don't know anything about him. But I've always been giving money to Svetlana for our son. It's the least I could do after the way I treated them."

"I see," Nikolai said.

"I'm really grateful for your help, Nikolai. This is a difficult time for me and the company." Pyotr Alekseevich paused and shook his head. "When I took over the company, I was ready for hard work and challenges, but I didn't expect things to get this dangerous. But I have to stay positive, right? At least, the pipeline problems are mostly solved. Pollution from oil spills could be another reason to shut us down or drown us in fines. But that's not your problem, Nikolai, sorry. You have enough to deal with."

"It's quite all right. I'm here to help," Nikolai said. "And the more information I have, the better I will be able to help you."

"There's something else you need to know," Pyotr Alekseevich said. "Remember that security guard who was killed in a jealous rage?"

"Sure. Anything new about it?"

"Yes. I don't think jealousy had anything to do with the murder."

"How so?" Nikolai said.

"The murdered guard was a night watchman. He walked the perimeter of the compound once an hour, with breaks in the security office in-between. He had a precise schedule. Every hour, he would walk for forty-five minutes and take a fifteen-minute break inside the security office. The night before he was killed, he dozed off during his scheduled fifteen-minute break. Slept for forty-five minutes, until another security guard came and woke him up. He went back outside, but his schedule was off, so we have reasons to suspect he ended up in the wrong place at the wrong time."

"But what about his affair with the other guy's wife? Is that no longer a possible motive for his murder?" Nikolai said.

"The investigators are not ruling it out, but it seems less likely, now that we know more details."

"What kind of details?" Nikolai said.

"The night of the murder, he was alone, in his own apartment, and his neighbor, the woman he was supposedly having an affair with, was working late. Since they were not together, the crime of passion theory doesn't quite work. There's another motive behind this murder, and I think that the real motive is related to his job as a night guard."

"Like what? He saw things he wasn't supposed to see when he went on his rounds? And somebody saw him and decided to get rid of him?" Nikolai said.

"That's what I think. I don't know what he saw. But whatever it was, it was obviously serious enough to warrant someone taking this man's life."

"That's important information. I'll have to do some investigating to find out what or whom he might have seen. What else do I need to know about?"

"About a few phone calls I've been getting." Pyotr Alekseevich pointed to the office phone. "Every time I get these calls, the message is the same. Sell the company or die."

"And you can't trace the calls or identify the voice, right?"

"That's right," Pyotr Alekseevich said. "And that's about it for now. Probably enough to keep you busy." He shook his head. "What a mess. Thank you again, Nikolai. If you need any other information, call me or stop by anytime. And if I learn anything new, I will let you know, of course."

As they were finishing the conversation, Natalya came into the office. She greeted Pyotr Alekseevich, ignored Nikolai, and sat down at her computer to type her translations.

After confirming with Pyotr Alekseevich that Natalya would stay in the office until he came back, Nikolai headed for the security office. He had a few things to discuss with Vanya.

Chapter Eight

Inside the security office, two young guards sat at the table chatting about the previous night's hockey game. When they saw Nikolai, they stopped talking, and greeted him politely. One of them immediately went outside, probably to do his rounds, the other moved to the desk with all the security monitors.

"Most of the cameras have been installed, but the monitors are still offline," the guard said. He looked at Nikolai. "Vanya knows, and he already called Oleg."

Nikolai nodded and stepped outside. He was getting used to the brisk chilly air and was even beginning to enjoy it. The air was so much clearer and cleaner here than in Moscow. Without the heavy foot and car traffic and the pollution of the big city, Upper Luzinsk's snow was whiter, fluffier, and purer. It reminded Nikolai of his college days and weekends he spent skiing with Olga and their friends at the dacha, his family's modest cottage outside of Moscow, with the cold and crisp days and cozy evenings by the fire. Those were simpler times of his youth that he sometimes longed for.

There was still no sign of Vanya, so Nikolai called Anatoly to check on the details of his replacement's arrival.

"Vasily Petrovich stopped by today," Anatoly said. "He knows the government lawyer who is coming to the meeting and doesn't trust him. That lawyer used to represent one of the major banks, and they worked together on the economy stabilization initiative."

"Sounds impressive, but I have no idea what that initiative was. Do I need to know?"

"Yes. The idea was that a bunch of big banks got together and offered loans to the government, ostensibly to help support the most critical areas for the economy, such as the oil and gas industry."

"You're talking about the time before these industries were privatized, right?" Nikolai said.

"Right. At the time, Luzinsk Oil and Gas was still government-owned," Anatoly said.

"So where's the catch? There is a catch, correct?"

"When banks and governments are involved, there's always a catch. Without cluttering your mind with all the details, I can tell you that the scheme worked basically like this: the government used Luzinsk Oil and Gas as collateral to get the loan and invested the money back into the industry, supposedly. And Luzinsk Oil and Gas was valued high, much too high, so the loan was high as well."

"Invested the money? Down some black hole?" Nikolai asked.

"Most likely. The officials probably bought yachts and mansions for themselves on the Mediterranean, on Cyprus, or in Florida. So, when the time came to repay the loan, the money was not there. And, miraculously enough, the value of Luzinsk Oil and Gas had dropped significantly right at that time."

"With some creative accounting?" Nikolai asked.

"Of course. So, the government could not repay the loan and was about to transfer ownership of Luzinsk Oil and Gas to the banks. And that's where Vasily Petrovich comes in. He discovered this creative accounting, saw through the whole scheme, had proof for it, and stopped the deal. So, Luzinsk Oil and Gas was never transferred to the bank and remained government property. Since everyone involved had their hands in embezzlement and misappropriation of funds, things got quiet for a while."

"That was before Pyotr Alekseevich took over?" Nikolai asked.

"Right. It was all under the old director, and that's when Vasily Petrovich, in his role as the government lawyer, started looking at the company's books more and saw evidence of tax evasion, too. Right after that, Pyotr Alekseevich took over as the director of the company. Soon after, the company went from being government-owned to private ownership. This was done legally, and the transition allowed the company to start public trading."

"But the fight is not over, right?"

"Right. If the tax repayment schedule is not finalized at the Board meeting, then Luzinsk Oil and Gas will be up for grabs. And there are plenty of people, including everyone involved in the previous dealings with the company, who want to grab it. Pyotr Alekseevich is the man this whole deal is hedging on. If he's out of the picture, many people will make a lot of money."

"So, is the old director still influencing things?"

"I'm sure he's involved somehow, despite being under investigation. From what Vasily Petrovich tells me, many influential people have their sights on Luzinsk Oil and would use any chance they have to get it. That makes sense, of course, since Luzinsk Oil has some rich oil fields, from what I hear."

"Anatoly, I don't think that just me and one other bodyguard for Natalya is enough here. We're dealing with bigger problems and need more support."

"I think you're right. Let me make a few phone calls, and I'll get back to you."

"Thanks," Nikolai said. He saw Vanya walking towards him. "I have to go, too. The local security director is here for a walk around. I'll let you know if we find something you need to know about."

Nikolai clicked off.

"Ready for our walk?" Vanya said.

"Let's check the monitors inside the security office first," Nikolai said. "You've had problems with the computer system, right?"

"Yes, but everything is fine now. Oleg fixed it," Vanya said.

"Do you know what the problems were?" Nikolai asked.

Vanya shook his head. "I don't know much about all this high-tech stuff. That's Oleg's job."

"I see," Nikolai said. "Can I take a look?"

"What, you don't believe me that everything is working?" Vanya said.

Nikolai did not respond.

For a second, Vanya looked at him, then reached for the doorknob. "Never mind.

Don't answer that. Let's go inside."

Nikolai followed Vanya into the security office and sat down at the desk. All the newly installed cameras were working, and the monitors flickered with inside images of Pyotr Alekseevich's office building, all the hallways, entryways, and stairwells. Outside the building, the cameras were mounted to show the driveway to the main gate and monitor the perimeter of the fence.

"Everything looks good," Nikolai said.

"I told you Oleg fixed it. And he did," Vanya said.

"Now let's take a walk to make sure that we're seeing all we need to see," Nikolai said.

"That gap with the wire wrapped around it is fixed if that's what you mean, so you should be happy," Vanya said.

"I'm still not thrilled about the cheap fence, but at least the cameras make it easier to monitor the perimeter."

They followed the path from the security building to the storage shed, to the piles of construction materials, through the areas where visitors and contractors parked their cars, and headed over to the engineering building. All the newly mounted cameras had their tiny green signal lights on, indicating that they were working, all the street lamps were lit, and the fence, however flimsy, had no more gaps or holes.

They took a few more steps, and the area around them grew darker. Nikolai stopped. "How often do your guys check the lights?" Nikolai pointed to two burnt-out street lamps next to the post where a surveillance camera had not been installed yet.

"Every night."

"So, both of these must have just burned out? Two at once?"

"Could be a coincidence." Vanya shrugged.

"I don't believe in coincidences," Nikolai said and pointed to the neat stack of roof panels placed between the two street lamps, right by the fence. "What are these panels for?"

"For the storage shed next to the garage. There was a leak there, and the roof needs to be fixed."

"That storage shed? All the way over there?" Nikolai pointed towards the garage by the main gate, a good three-minute walk away. "Why are the roof panels here? Another coincidence?"

Vanya shook his head. "The delivery guys just put them here. How were they supposed to know what these roof panels are for?"

"Wasn't one of your guards supervising the delivery?" Nikolai said.

"They should have."

"That's not what I asked," Nikolai said. "Was the delivery supervised or not?"

"How in the world do I know?" Vanya said, his tone defensive now. "I can't keep track of every little thing around here."

"Obviously not," Nikolai muttered under his breath. "Let's move the panels over and check out the area under them."

"It's just roof panels. Not the best place to store them, but how dangerous can they be?"

"That's exactly what I want to find out. Give me a hand here," Nikolai said.

Reluctantly, Vanya walked over to the stack of panels. One by one, Nikolai and Vanya moved all the panels over to the side, revealing a snow-free dark spot on the ground.

"Hand me the flashlight," Nikolai said to Vanya. He pointed the light at the dark patch. "Somebody has been busy here."

The light revealed a cave-like opening next to the fence. It looked deep and wide enough for an average-sized person to squeeze in. But why would anybody want to squeeze into a hole in the ground?

Nikolai shone his light into the hole. The ray of his flashlight bounced off the well-packed snow on all sides of the hole. Then, he saw something.

"Vanya, it's a tunnel. I can see some trees on the other side."

Vanya crouched down next to Nikolai. "You think it's the thieves again, trying to get the roof panels this time?" Vanya said. "This stuff can be expensive, you know. And with all the snowfall around here, many roofs need frequent repair."

"I don't think so. The roof panels are too big to fit in there. It's barely wide enough for a person to fit through."

"Right," Vanya said. "I didn't think of that. Still thinking of those stolen construction material some weeks ago."

"Something different is going on here. Let's see if we can figure out what."

Nikolai got on all fours and started working his way through the tunnel, tightly packed snow surrounding him on all sides. The awkward movement made his leg ache, but Nikolai ignored the pain. It was just soreness, nothing serious.

Vanya followed.

Digging a tunnel through the frozen earth and snow could not have been easy and must have required a lot of effort and some special equipment. How could that project have gone unnoticed? With one last push, Nikolai was on the other side.

Breathing heavily, Vanya stood up next to him. "I've never been a fan of tight spaces. How did they even manage to dig it through the frozen earth?" He shook the snow off his coat and stretched his back.

"That's what I'm wondering, too. And how could it be that nobody has seen any activity here?"

"Maybe somebody did see it, but they didn't tell us," Vanya said.

"And when are these panels supposed to be used?" Nikolai said.

"I don't know."

"I bet it's after the Board meeting, and whoever made this tunnel knows it," Nikolai said.

"How do you figure that?"

"Because whoever dug this tunnel surely does not want these roof panels moved and the tunnel discovered before the Board meeting."

"Makes sense," Vanya said.

"Help me get oriented here," Nikolai said. "Where's the main road?"

"Pretty close. See that old pine tree? That's where the dirt road starts that leads to the main road out of town," Vanya said.

"And once they are out of town, they are home free. They can go to the airport or the train station. With the non-existent security in both places, they can sneak onto a freight train or even board the daily charter to Moscow," Nikolai said. "Or a helicopter anywhere they want to go, especially if they know the local pilots."

"It's possible." Vanya nodded.

"So, let's say this is a getaway tunnel then."

"You mean, the murderer plans to come in through the main gate and then leave through the tunnel?" Vanya said.

"I think so. And it can also be used to bring stuff in," Nikolai said.

"Like what stuff?" Vanya said.

"Something small enough to fit through it."

"Not roof panels, I'd guess," Vanya said.

Nikolai chuckled. "You're catching on quickly."

"You think the death threats and this tunnel are related?"

Nikolai nodded. "Pretty sure."

"So whoever is trying to kill Pyotr Alekseevich or his two Board members will use this tunnel to come in or to bring their murder weapons in?"

"That's a possibility. Let's think logically. There are many ways to kill somebody. Which would be the method of choice here?"

Vanya shook his head. "Anything, really, from poisoning to drug overdose, anything at all, right?"

"Not necessarily. If the tunnel is used to smuggle something into the compound, then we can probably exclude poisons and other substances, right? We don't check for those at the gate, so why bother digging a tunnel?"

"As a getaway, you said it yourself."

"But a getaway would not be needed in case of poisoning or drug overdose. Most poisons and drugs take some time to take effect, and some more time for those effects to be discovered, so our murderer could just walk out the front gate, right?" Nikolai said.

"I guess so," Vanya said.

"The way I see it, the most likely possibility is a firearms attack. That's what you check for at the gate, right?"

Vanya nodded. "And we have been searching all cars coming in for weapons."

"And the murderers, whoever they are, know that. That's why they need the tunnel, to bring the firearms in."

"That makes our job a little easier and narrows down the possibilities, right? We just need to watch out for firearms," Vanya said.

Nikolai thought for a moment. "I bet that whoever is planning to kill Pyotr Alekseevich or the two Board members is already inside the compound. The question is who it is."

Chapter Nine

For a few minutes, Nikolai and Vanya stood next to the tunnel. Nikolai kept shining his flashlight into the twilight around them.

"What are you looking for?" Vanya said.

"I'll know it when I see it," Nikolai said.

He peered into the dark tundra trying to see something that could give him a clue. Any clue. Then, a group of trees caught his eye. "Not much of a clue, but I see it," he said.

"What? I don't see anything."

"Whoever made this tunnel made sure that it was well-hidden," Nikolai said shining his flashlight towards the trees. "See these three dwarf trees?"

"What about them?"

"They are not growing here. They have been moved from somewhere else and stuck in the snow."

"Why do you think that?" Vanya said.

"Look around. All the other trees are leaning every which way, and these three are perfectly straight, like they are not affected by the permafrost layers melting and freezing," Nikolai said.

"That's right. I didn't even think about it," Vanya said. "Good point."

"Thanks. Anyway, enough forestry discussions. And it's not much of a discovery anyway. It's not surprising that whoever built this tunnel tried to hide it. I don't think we'll find anything else, so let's go before someone finds us."

"Should we close it? The tunnel?" Vanya said. "Mess up their plans?"

"No. We should leave it as is. We have a clear point in our favor here: the killers had a secret, and we discovered it.

Now we have the knowledge they don't suspect we have, and we can use it to our advantage."

"So, just install a new camera then?"

"Only if that was a part of the original security plan. We don't know who is involved, so we shouldn't do anything that could arouse anyone's suspicions,"

Nikolai said. "Let's go back into the compound and put those panels back where they were."

Nikolai bent down and started squeezing back through the cold and dark tunnel. A few moments later, they were on the other side. They quickly loaded the roof panels back in their spot, covering the entrance to the tunnel.

"Shall I tell the guys not to replace the lights?" Vanya said. "That way, we won't arouse any suspicions."

"Don't tell anybody anything," Nikolai said. "First, we don't know who we're up against, so alerting anyone to our knowledge is not a good idea. Second, it's best to keep the routine as it always has been. Let your guys discover that the lights are out and replace them as they see fit, like they always do."

"You're a smart one, aren't you?" Vanya said. "You really think everything through."

"It's just experience and training," Nikolai said as they two of them continued their walk. "I've been dealing with these kinds of things for a while now."

"How long have you been doing this work?"

"Just over three years."

"You learned a lot in a short time," Vanya said.

"It's a question of survival. Moscow has not been the safest place lately. Free enterprise tends to come at a high price. Of course, that's why I have this job."

"Right." Vanya thought for a moment, then asked, "So, what's our next task?"

"Pyotr Alekseevich promised to leave some files in your security office for me. I'd like to look through them and see if we find anything that can give us any clues."

"Look through the files? I thought you were a bodyguard, not a detective."

"I have to be both. Detectives are reactive and investigate after a crime has been committed. Bodyguards have to prevent crimes, so we have to be proactive and stop crimes before they happen. It's our job. We have to do anything we can to accomplish that purpose, including sort through paper files."

Back in the security office, Vanya put on the tea kettle and turned on the space heater.

"Thanks," Nikolai said. "I need that after crawling through the tunnel."

"Me too," Vanya said.

Nikolai opened a large box labeled with his name that Pyotr Alekseevich left for him. The box was filled with papers, files, maps, and other various materials.

Nikolai started sorting through it. For a while, nothing caught his eye: there were old minutes of various meetings, maps and blueprints of sections of the oil field, summer and winter routes between wells, and pages of technical notes written in barely discernible handwriting.

Vanya put a cup of steaming tea on the desk next to the box.

"Thanks," Nikolai took a sip and kept sorting. He glanced at his watch. It was getting late in the day, and he needed to talk to Pyotr Alekseevich before the director headed to another meeting or home for the day. Nikolai picked up one more paper. It was a printed page that looked like a guest list. Clipped to it was a draft of an old invitation to a corporate picnic. Nikolai looked at it closely as something caught his attention.

"An old picnic invitation?" Vanya glanced at the page.

"And a guest list." He handed the page to Vanya. "Read the names of this couple." Nikolai pointed to a line on the guest list. "The woman's last name is the same as the old director's. Are they related?"

Vanya nodded. "She's is the old director's sister. I don't know much about them. They lived in Moscow and rarely came here."

"Are they still in Moscow? What do they do there?"

"Not sure about the woman, but her husband is a big shot in some company that owns a bunch of other companies." Vanya thought for a moment. "As a matter of fact, I remember him talking about buying Luna Oil and Gas some months ago."

Nikolai looked at the husband's name: D.F. Petrenko.

"Do you know his first name?" Nikolai said.

Vanya furrowed his brows, looked at the initials, then at Nikolai. "Dmitry Fedorovich, I think, or Denis Fedorovich, something like that."

"Do you happen to know the name of his company?" Nikolai said.

"No, not off-hand. I could check."

Nikolai looked at the invitation and the names again. "Actually, don't worry about it. Not important." Nikolai knew exactly who could find all the information he needed. He was about to excuse himself to go make the call, but his cell phone buzzed.

It was Anatoly.

"Any news?" Nikolai asked after he stepped outside and started walking to Pyotr Alekseevich's office. The wind was blowing snow in all directions, obscuring the path and getting into Nikolai's face. He picked up his pace, walked inside the building, and stopped by the staircase. He wanted to finish this conversation before heading back up.

"As we expected, the old director is putting pressure on Pyotr Alekseevich to sell the company," Anatoly said. "But you already knew that."

"Right," Nikolai said. "So what's the real news?"

"The company's financial problems go well beyond the unpaid taxes. Apparently, the old director made deliberate attempts to bankrupt the company so he could sell it at a low price to himself."

"Care to explain that part?" Nikolai said.

"He set up another company, with a different corporate name and a different bank account. And that's the company that is trying to buy Luzinsk Oil and Gas."

"I see," Nikolai said.

"But Pyotr Alekseevich is determined to stay in charge of Luzinsk Oil and Gas, and he's about to sign a deal with the government to that effect."

"I know that," Nikolai said. "That's why I'm here. And that all is supposed to happen by the end of the Board meeting. Next week."

"Right. So, what I get from this whole story is that if the deal is not signed by then," Anatoly continued, "the company will go on sale. Cheaply. Is that how you understand it, too?"

"Yes."

"And there's only one condition that could stop Pyotr Alekseevich and the other two Board members from signing the deal." Anatoly paused.

"If one of them dies," Nikolai said.

"I'm afraid so. I'm sending reinforcement from the agency tomorrow, as Pyotr Alekseevich has asked for. Get ready to meet them."

"Can you also send Viktor? Can you spare him for a day or so?" Nikolai said.

"Viktor the computer guy? Why?"

"The company seems to have a lot of computer problems, including computers that operate security cameras and monitors. I want to make sure nothing fishy's going on."

"Don't they have a computer person?" Anatoly said.

"Sure, they do. But I don't know if I trust him."

"Got it. I'll send Viktor," Anatoly said and clicked off.

A blast of freezing arctic wind sent a chill through Nikolai's bones despite the warm parka he was wearing, but it was not time to go inside yet. He had one more phone call to make.

Chapter Ten

Nikolai punched the number into his phone, and Olga picked up right away.

"I have something to ask you," Nikolai said.

"Not about my promotion, I hope. I'm beginning to suspect you're just envious that I'll be making more money than you. Male ego problems?"

"Maybe, a little of that," Nikolai said. He was a little taken aback by Olga's harsh tone, but decided this was no time to argue. He had a job to do. "What is Denis Fedorovich's last name?"

"Petrenko."

"That's what I suspected."

"What is that supposed to mean?"

Nikolai paused, then told her everything he had discovered about Denis Fedorovich and his company. Olga listened without interrupting him, so Nikolai could not tell what her reaction was to all this new information.

"Now that you know all this," Nikolai said. "Can you promise me not to accept his job offer?"

"Promise you?" Olga said. "I don't know if you're telling me all that because you want to protect me, or because you're jealous of my promotion. Let's face it: I make more money than you do, my schedule is easier, and I get better job offers and promotions. You are just a servant, nothing else. And there's one more thing. I'm moving out."

"You're what?" Nikolai did not expect this reaction from Olga. "Moving out?"

"We both know that our relationship is not working, so why waste any more time on it. It's better if I just move out."

"You don't want to wait till I come back so we can talk about it in person?"

"There's nothing to talk about. Nothing you can say will change my mind."

"All right," Nikolai said. Olga's words hurt, and he still loved her, despite all the recent problems and disagreements. At the same time, he felt a sense of relief. Olga was right. She was saying exactly what Nikolai had been thinking for a while but never had the courage to bring up. "I'm sorry things did not work out for us."

"Just like that?" Olga said. "You're giving up that quickly? I knew you never loved me. I'll leave the key on the kitchen table."

Before Nikolai could say anything else, Olga clicked off. For a moment, Nikolai contemplated calling her back but decided not to. What could he tell her? That he used to love her but the social and political circumstances of their changing country and of their lives erased his love for her? Or erased the person Olga used to be? All that would sound like pathetic excuses, especially over the phone. It was better just to let her move out and have a longer conversation in person, after Nikolai got back to Moscow, if Olga would even want to have such a conversation.

Nikolai closed his eyes for a second, exhaled, and put the phone away. Then, he stepped into the warmth of the office building, climbed up the steps and stopped outside of Pyotr Alekseevich's office. The door was open, and Nikolai could hear the director's agitated voice.

"Yes, I got the report," Pyotr Alekseevich was saying. "The numbers are incredibly high. Yes, of course, we're checking. We've been checking day and night since we got the information from MENDAX Environmental Group. Yes, they are our new consultants. And no, we can't find the source of the problem. It may be a leak in one of the underground pipes. Yes, of course, we'll keep looking. We are looking."

Nikolai stepped into the office. Pyotr Alekseevich stood by the window, tapping a pencil on the glass. Isolated from the outside world by her ear buds, Natalya was at the computer, typing busily.

"Problems?" Nikolai said.

Pyotr Alekseevich turned to him and nodded. "Serious ones. We got the environmental report, and it shows high contamination of soil and water, and that means a major leak in the pipeline."

"But isn't the pipeline new?" Nikolai said.

"It is. But things can happen even with a new pipeline," Pyotr Alekseevich said.

"Especially if somebody wants them to happen."

"You're thinking sabotage?" Nikolai said.

"I'm not ruling it out." Pyotr Alekseevich said. "But whatever the reason, we can't even find that leak. That's really bad news, especially just before the Board meeting. The government could just close us down, and auction off our assets." He shook his head, then walked over to Natalya and tapped her on the shoulder lightly. She pulled out her ear buds and looked up.

"I need to go back to the oil field," Pyotr Alekseevich said. "Could you please stay here and work on these documents?" He handed her a folder.

A moment later, Nikolai's phone buzzed. It was Vanya.

"Your guys are here," Vanya said. "Can you come to the front gate to help me identify them? There's enough manpower here to take over a small country, so you'd better make sure these guys are on our side."

"You're learning fast," Nikolai said. "I'll be right there."

A minivan was parked outside the main gate. Nikolai nodded to Vanya and walked out of the compound to the van. He greeted the driver, a dark-haired young man, but did not recognize him.

"Mind if I look inside?" Nikolai said.

"Go ahead," the driver said and opened the passenger door.

Nikolai leaned in. He saw Andrei, his buddy from training, and Viktor, Centurion's computer expert, next to Andrei. He recognized the other four men as well. Nikolai greeted them, stepped away from the van, motioned for Vanya to open the gate, and walked back inside the compound.

"Anatoly sent our computer guy, too. Mind if he takes a look at your system?" Nikolai said.

"But we have Oleg," Vanya said.

"As they say, two heads are better than one," Nikolai said.

Vanya shook his head. "Right. I know what you're doing. You don't trust anyone, do you?"

"Trust but verify. Anyway, why don't you have Viktor check the network, and you take the guys to the hotel. Meanwhile, I'll talk to Andrei, my replacement," Nikolai said. "Once you're done at the hotel, bring them back, and we'll chat."

"All right. I guess I'm no longer in charge." Vanya opened the door of the van and climbed inside. Two young men jumped out, and the van took off towards the hotel.

Both men were dressed in thick dark-colored parkas, big boots, and fur hats, but even in these similar outfits, the differences in their appearances were starkly obvious. Andrei, Nikolai's replacement, was short and stocky, with dark curly hair. Viktor, the computer expert, was tall and slender. As he came out of the van, Viktor adjusted his fashionable rimless glasses and pulled on his gloves.

He worked hard and was well-compensated for the late nights and the long hours, and that explained his expensive tastes, in his outfits and in his choices of exotic vacations. He loved spending time somewhere on warm beaches in Turkey, Spain, or Greece, and his affinity for warm weather was indicated by his tanned face, a sharp contrast to the infinite whiteness around them.

"Not my favorite climate," Viktor said. "Next time you have computer problems, can you have them in a Monaco casino or somewhere in the Mediterranean?"

"I'll do my best," Nikolai said.

"I bet Nikolai doesn't mind this job, despite the freezing weather," Andrei said. "Guarding a young girl. What a cushy assignment. I bet she's pretty, too."

"Not my type," Nikolai said. "Let's go chat while Viktor checks the network. I want to tell you more about Natalya and this whole assignment."

"I hope the computers are someplace warm," Viktor said. "I hate this cold."

The three of them walked inside the security office. Nikolai handed Viktor a piece of paper. "All the network passwords are here. Make sure to destroy this information after you're done."

"Yes, boss," Viktor said. "I'll eat it, just like spies do in the movies." He chuckled. "I've got all I need, so just give me an hour or so."

Nikolai and Andrei stepped outside and started walking the perimeter of the fence. The weather was freezing cold, as always, but at least the wind had died down, allowing Nikolai and Andrei to talk without blowing snow blinding them.

"I'm listening," Andrei said, putting his gloved hands deeper into his pockets. "Tell me all I need to know."

"In a minute. First, tell me how you've been," Nikolai said. "I haven't seen you for a while. Busy?"

"Pretty busy," Andrei said without looking at Nikolai.

"What assignments have you been on? Worked with anyone I might know?"

"I've been away, you know," Andrei said.

"Away where?"

For a moment Andrei was quiet, with only the crunching of their footsteps on the snow breaking the silence. "I'm not too proud of what had happened," Andrei finally said, "but Anatoly told me to make sure you know. Just in case."

"What is it?" Nikolai wondered if Andrei got himself into some legal trouble over a client.

"I just couldn't get my life back on track after my wife died. I started missing work, then got into drinking, and everything was just falling apart. If it weren't for Anatoly, I don't know where I would be right now. Probably dead. Anatoly pretty much forced me to get into rehab for alcohol. He saved my life."

"I'm glad you're better, Andrei," Nikolai said. Of course, Nikolai remembered the car accident that killed Andrei's wife, but he also remembered Andrei getting back to work after it, and then Nikolai got so involved with his own work and with Olga that he lost track of Andrei. Now, he felt a twinge of guilt.

Andrei was not a close friend, but he was a colleague, and Nikolai should have at least called him on the phone.

"I'm, too. It was tough for a while."

"I am sorry to hear it," Nikolai said. "Anatoly always told me he was keeping you busy, and I never questioned him. I just thought you were working."

"That's fine," Andrei said. "We all get busy, and Anatoly knew more than anyone else in the company since he's in charge. He's a good guy. He left it up to me to tell you what really happened. So, now you know."

"How are you now?"

"Much better, "Andrei said. "I'm fine. It's all in the past. I learned how to handle stress without drinking, so you don't have to worry about me. What about you? Are you and Olga married? Any kids yet?"

"No to both. That's not happening. As they say, our life is like a fairy-tale: the further we go, the scarier it gets."

"I thought you really liked each other. What went wrong?"

"Olga is great. It's me. I have a hard time adjusting to all these changes, to her new career, to the fancy functions she attends. And our job, as you well know, is not too conducive to family life." As soon as Nikolai said these last words, he regretted them. Andrei was doing just fine with his family life until his wife died. "I'm sorry, Andrei. I was just talking about myself. I didn't mean to include you in that statement. Sorry."

"I know what you meant, buddy. Don't apologize," Andrei said. "How's your recovery going?"

"I'm pretty much back to normal. The wounded leg aches once in a while, but not enough to prevent me from doing what I need to do."

"I'm glad to hear that," Andrei said. "So, we're both back to normal now. That's good to know. And it's good to see you again."

"You, too."

They were almost half-way around the compound. The street lamps were all working, and the cameras were glowing with their tiny green lights.

"So, tell me about this Natalya and what my job is," Andrei said.

"Natalya's pretty smart and hard-working, despite what her dad led me to believe," Nikolai said. "She has an English degree and works as an interpreter for Pyotr Alekseevich, the company's director."

"And why does she need a bodyguard?"

"Up until now, she really did not. It was just her dad's way to have somebody watch over her and keep her out of trouble. Since money is no issue for him, he contacted our company, and I got the job. But now that the situation around Pyotr Alekseevich is getting pretty tense, some extra protection for Natalya couldn't hurt."

"Makes sense. Is she easy to work with?"

"Not too bad. I'll introduce you as soon as I show you something."

Nikolai led Andrei around the perimeter of the fence, past the security building, past all the office buildings, and to the area where he and Vanya had discovered the tunnel. The two lamp posts had new lights in them now, and they were shining down on the stack of metal roof panels and the fence beyond them.

"See these roof panels?" Nikolai said. "There's a tunnel under them."

"A tunnel? In this freezing ground? Any idea how long it's been here?"

"I couldn't tell by looking at it, but the panels here are recent, so I'd venture to say that the tunnel hasn't been here for too long. I bet it's a gift for the Board meeting."

"Anything inside there?" Andrei asked and came closer.

"Nothing."

Nikolai shone his flashlight around the panels but could not spot any signs of recent activity, then came up to the fence and peered at the other side. In the permanent darkness that was Upper Luzinsk's arctic winter, it was hard to discern much. The three trees that he noticed before were still there and still as straight as before, and there were no discernible footprints or tire tracks in the snow. Of course, even if somebody had been there, on foot or in a vehicle, all the traces would have been erased by the previous night's snowfall.

"As far as I can tell, everything is the way Vanya and I had left it, so I don't think anybody has been here," Nikolai said. "Of course, they don't need to come here now. It's a getaway route, and there's nothing to get away from yet. So, that's what I wanted to show you. Shall we head back?"

"And who are they, these people who made the tunnel? You don't have any leads, do you?" Andrei said.

"None," Nikolai said. "Hired help, as Anatoly calls them. Contract killers."

"I figured that much," Andrei said.

They stepped away from the fence and started walking back.

"What's going on here?" they heard Natalya's voice. "We're all preparing for this big meeting, and you're going for walks? Nothing better to do?"

She was walking towards them, a big white scarf wrapped around her, her long fur coat almost touching the snow. Her hands, thick mittens on them, were swinging freely, adding to a glamorous and carefree look. To Nikolai, she looked out of place in this not-so-glamorous town and in stark contrast to his and Andrei's serious mood.

"We were just checking on these roof panels," Nikolai said. "Vanya thought somebody was trying to steal them the other night. The real question is what are you doing here, Natalya? And how did you know we were here?"

She shrugged. "I didn't know. I was bored, so I just followed you guys here."

"Doesn't Pyotr Alekseevich need your help?" Nikolai said.

"Not now. He's meeting with some regional bosses, and they all speak Russian."

"All right. Please don't follow us again. It could be dangerous. But since you're here, let me introduce you to your new bodyguard, Andrei."

"Pleasure to meet you," Andrei said.

Natalya smiled. "You look like you've been in this job for a while," she said to Andrei as the three of them headed back to Pyotr Alekseevich's office. "You don't seem as uptight as Nikolai here."

"Appearances can be deceptive," Andrei said.

"Maybe so," Natalya said. "So tell me, how did you get into this job?"

"First you tell me how you got a job here. Isn't this a boring place for a young pretty woman? All darkness and snow, and not even a movie theater for entertainment?" Andrei said.

"A job is a job, and this one pays well. Many times more than a similar job in Moscow if I could even get one there. Not many people want to come all the way here, you know."

"Like you really need the money," Nikolai said.

"I don't want to take my dad's money anymore. I want to make my own and spend it the way I want to," Natalya said. "After this job is done, I'm going to Cyprus. Warm water, sunny days, the beach. I want to learn scuba-diving."

"Sounds nice," Andrei said. "How long are you staying here?"

"As long as I need," Natalya said. "Now tell me about yourself, Andrei. How did you become a bodyguard?"

"Do you really want to know or are you just making conversation?" Andrei asked.

"I really want to know. I've never met any bodyguards before, besides you and Nikolai, and I'm curious."

"All right, I'll tell you," Andrei said. "I was planning to go to college to study engineering but didn't get enough points to get in, so, like all other young guys, I was drafted into the military. While serving my two years, I kept reading engineering and math books in the little free time that I had. I was really determined to get into an engineering school. But then something changed, and I lost interest in all that."

"Why?" Natalya asked. "What happened?"

"The 1991 August coup happened and it changed everything. The division I served in was sent to the Russian Parliament building where President Yeltsin was working on a plan to resist the coup. At first, when our division got called to the building, I thought we were supposed to support Yeltsin, bring democracy back, and all those lofty kinds of things. I was proud to be there even though the orders were not clear: they told us to surround the building and just maintain order. Still, that made sense to me: thousands of Yeltsin supporters gathered in front of the building, everyone was agitated, and when nerves are on edge in a big crowd, all kinds of dangerous things can happen. So, I completely understood and accepted the assignment. But as the day progressed, I saw the conflict between the coup leaders and Yeltsin get more and more serious. And I also realized that the orders we got were from the coup leaders, not from Yeltsin's group. By the evening, there was talk of storming the building. And do you know what that meant?"

"What?" Natalya asked.

"It meant that we, the soldiers, would have to shoot our own people, Muscovites like us. There was no way I was going to do it. The military is supposed to protect its people from external enemies, not shoot them. And, of course, you know what happened next, right?"

"Sure," Natalya said. "I was little but I remember how happy my parents were when the soldiers and all the tanks sent to the Parliament disobeyed their military orders from the coup leaders and joined Yeltsin's defenders."

Andrei nodded. "Yes, and that's exactly what we did, with all our tanks."

"When we heard the news, we were all cheering and eating ice-cream. My mom always told me that the support of the military was the deciding factor in the outcome of the coup. If you guys weren't that brave, who knows where we would be now."

"In Siberia, probably, in some labor camp," Andrei said. "Working all day for a bowl of soup."

Nikolai chuckled. "And now we're even farther than Siberia, but at least we are working for money."

"But I still don't understand how that coup made you want to become a bodyguard, Andrei," Natalya said.

"I've always thought of myself as a patriot, but I only realized what that really meant during those days and nights of the August coup. Before, I was thinking about myself, my engineering studies, my future. I was limited to my own world and did not even know it. And when I was at the Parliament building, with all those people around me who came there out of their own free will because they wanted to see a better future for our country, I felt that I needed to protect them, to defend them. I was ready to die for them because of the ideals they had and of the hopes they were trying to fulfill. Not their own little individual hopes, but hopes of the whole country. It was at that moment that I realized that protecting each person or even just one person is the highest form of patriotism. To be a patriot, you need to believe in what you're defending and know what or who you're defending. The job of a bodyguard, protecting one specific client from harm, felt like the ultimate form of patriotism to me."

"Deep stuff," Nikolai said, and he meant it. Many of the things Andrei was saying were things that Nikolai felt himself. He just never took the time to put them in words.

Natalya was quietly listening.

As they were walking towards the building, they passed by some old tree stumps next to a patch of young trees.

Andrei stopped. "See these stumps?"

Natalya and Nikolai stopped as well.

"Sure we see them," Natalya said. "What about them?"

"Life of a bodyguard is just like these trees. While you're young, you're high above the ground, the sun shines on you, gives you warmth, but then, there's a point in a bodyguard's life when he gets cut down."

Andrei patted one of the stumps. "And somewhere deep inside, life leaves holes, just like these ones." He picked at the rotten wood inside one of the stumps. It crumbled in his fingers.

"So, are you saying that you are like one of these stumps?" Natalya said.

"Not yet, but my time will come. One day, I will be too old to do this job, and I will be thrown aside, like these stumps. That's life. But you know what's worse than these stumps? It's what's not here, what we don't see. It's the young guys who perished while doing their duty, on the job, and not even an old stump was left to remind others of their big sacrifice. Life is a little more stable now, less dangerous even for bodyguards, but remember the nineties?"

Natalya nodded. "What about the nineties?"

"All through the nineties, there was so much crime, so many deaths of bodyguards who were killed while protecting their clients. And the newspapers did not write about these guys. There were no elaborate funerals or memorial services, no fancy monuments, nothing. Don't you agree, Nikolai? You know how most clients treat their bodyguards."

Nikolai shook his head. "But Andrei, it's a job, the clients don't owe us anything beyond the contract. It's a dangerous job, but we chose to do it, so we really shouldn't expect any extra gratitude or extra attention. Our job is to be gray shadows of our clients, unseen and unheard, remember?"

"Gray shadows or not, we are still people. And unlike shadows, we get hurt, we bleed and we die," Andrei said to Nikolai, then turned to Natalya. "Sorry, I got a little too philosophical here. You must be freezing. Why don't we go back inside."

"Good idea," Nikolai said. "Pyotr Alekseevich is probably back from his meeting and looking for you, Natalya."

As Nikolai watched Natalya, accompanied by Andrei, head towards Pyotr Alekseevich's building, he wondered if he had misjudged her. Sure, she was a little immature but she did not seem to be out of control or evil, like her dad made him and Anatoly believe. She was just young. But, like Nikolai's grandmother used to say, youth is a drawback that goes away with time. Natalya had plenty of time to become more mature and more serious.

When the heavy door slammed shut behind Natalya and Andrei, Nikolai chuckled, remembering Natalya's words about the sunny beaches of Cyprus. That image was especially appealing here and now, in this frozen arctic darkness. Nikolai braced himself for another burst of cold wind and headed to the security office where Viktor was working on the network.

"Did you find anything?" Nikolai asked him.

"Yes. Somebody infected the system with a variation of the JS-67 virus."

"What does it do?"

"Slows down the computers by taking up hard disk space, network storage space, and memory. There are a number of JS-67 versions. Some are malicious and can steal data and corrupt the system, others are just pranks. "

"Which one do we have?"

"I'll have to run some more checks back in the Moscow office but this one looks pretty harmless." Viktor took the flash drive out of the computer. "All I need is here. I'll let you know tomorrow."

"What's its origin? Did it come from the Internet?"

"No. The system has all the latest anti-virus software, with firewalls and automatic updates enabled, and JS-67 has been around for a while, so it would have been recognized by the anti-virus software and blocked from entry into the system. Someone put it in on purpose."

"But who would do that? And why?"

"Who has network passwords?"

"You, me, and Pyotr Alekseevich, the company's director," Nikolai said.

"You think he could be doing something?" Viktor said.

"Pyotr Alekseevich? Definitely not. Why would he?" Nikolai said. "He'd be hurting his own company. Plus, he doesn't seem to know that much about computers."

"Who does computer work around here?"

Nikolai shook his head. "Of course!" he exclaimed. "That was really dumb of me. Oleg, the local computer guy has all the passwords, and he has been working on all computers. He seems to be really good at making them speed up."

"So, he knows how to find the virus and how to remove it," Viktor said. "He probably also knows how to put it in. You need to talk to him. He knows more than he lets on."

"I will call him and Vanya right now."

Chapter Eleven

Barely twenty minutes after Nikolai's call, Oleg walked in, took off his mittens, and hung his coat on the rack by the door. "Computer problems? What's going on?" He smiled at Nikolai and Vanya and headed towards the desk with all the security monitors on it.

"That's exactly what we would like to know," Vanya said. "Have a seat." He pointed to a chair next to a small table in the corner. "We need to talk."

Oleg sat down, his carefree expression quickly disappearing.

Vanya sat down across from him. Nikolai leaned against the wall next to Vanya.

"We know what you've been up to," Nikolai said. "Tell us who hired you."

"What do you mean? Pyotr Alekseevich hired me," Oleg said.

"What are you up to, Oleg?" Vanya said, moving his chair closer to the table and leaning forward. "Tell us the truth."

"I just fix computers," Oleg said, his tone pleading and his eyes darting from Vanya to Nikolai.

"What other companies do you work for?" Nikolai said.

"Just this one and Luna Oil. Those are the only two in town."

"Luna Oil? And how much do they pay you?" Nikolai said.

"My rates are the same for both. It's all hourly. Why do you ask?"

"Just curious." Nikolai paused, trying to catch Oleg off-guard. "Tell me about JS-67."

"I don't know anything about it." Oleg shifted in the chair, his eyes focused on his tightly clasped hands on his lap.

"Have you ever removed JS-67 virus from the network?" Nikolai said.

"Sure."

"So you do know about it?" Vanya said.

"I know enough to remove it," Oleg said.

"How does the virus get into the network?" Nikolai said.

"Like all viruses, through Internet searches and such."

"Aren't you responsible for all anti-virus software? Don't you keep it up to date?" Nikolai said. "Oleg, look at me!"

Vanya leaned back, letting Nikolai ask the questions.

"Of course, I do," Oleg said, looking up at Nikolai.

"And is JS-67 a new virus?"

"No, it's not new. It's been around for a while."

"Then how can it get past all the latest anti-virus protections and firewalls?"

"I don't know."

"You should know. You run all the security checks and updates, right?" Nikolai said.

Oleg nodded, looking down at his hands again.

"And you have all the network passwords?"

Oleg nodded again.

"So you should know."

"There's nothing to know. I just come when they call me, run the tests, and fix whatever needs to be fixed. And sometimes I find that virus, JS-67, and I remove it."

Nikolai took a chair, flipped it around, and sat down right across from Oleg. "Listen to me. And look at me."

Oleg looked up again, fear and worry evident in his eyes.

"We can settle this issue here, and nicely," Nikolai continued. "Or you could go to jail for a long time. A very long time. And then your life here will seem like paradise."

"I really don't know."

"Fine." Nikolai sat back and turned to Vanya. "Call the police. Tell them we have a network security breach."

Vanya got up and walked to the phone on his desk.

"No, no, don't call. Please!" Oleg said.

"We've wasted enough time with you. You can explain it to the police. I'm sure they'll be interested," Nikolai said, getting up.

Vanya picked up the phone and started dialing.

"All right, all right," Oleg said. "It was me, but I swear I didn't do any harm. That virus doesn't do anything bad."

"And the virus doesn't collect data or copy files? Or corrupt files?" Nikolai said. He was now standing over Oleg, looking down at him.

"It doesn't, I swear. It just slows down the computers."

"So you put it into the computers on purpose, to slow them down?"

"Yes, but I didn't think it was a big deal."

"But why would you do that?"

Oleg paused, clearly embarrassed. "So I get called back to come work on them. It's hard to make money here, you know."

"And why should we believe you?" Nikolai said.

"Because I'm telling the truth." He looked at Nikolai. "My wife is pregnant, and we need the money. She won't be able to work for a while. Please don't call the police!"

Oleg's mention of his pregnant wife brought back Nikolai's first conversation with Oleg, back in the car when he was driving Nikolai and Natalya from the airport when they first came to Upper Luzinsk. That part was true, but what was also true that when people got desperate for money, like Oleg seemed to be, they were willing to bend or break the rules in many ways, probably more serious ones than putting an innocuous computer virus into the network. Nikolai motioned for Vanya to hang up.

"You're in trouble, Oleg, and you'd better be telling the truth," Nikolai said.

"If we find out that you're lying to us, you'll be in really big trouble."

"Can I go?" Oleg said.

"For now you can," Vanya said. "But don't even think of leaving town. We will be watching you. And I will let Pyotr Alekseevich know about this virus thing."

Oleg grabbed his coat and hat off the rack and rushed outside. Through the window, Nikolai watched him hurry off as he struggled to put his coat on in the freezing wind.

"I don't trust him," Nikolai said. "What do you think?"

"The only thing I know for sure is that his wife is pregnant, and they need the money," Vanya said.

"How much does he know?"

"He runs all kinds of errands for us, and probably for Luna Oil." Vanya paused.

"He listens to conversations in both companies and he's obviously not above some cheating."

"But how far would he go to get the money, do you think?" Nikolai said. "Could he be involved in that tunnel business?"

"I don't have much experience with all this intricate stuff. I'm mostly just a plain old security guard." Vanya paused. "But he doesn't look like a murderer to me."

"And what does a murderer look like?" Nikolai said.

"I don't know. I don't know anything anymore."

"We'll know more tomorrow, after Viktor runs more checks," Nikolai said.

"Right." Vanya nodded.

Nikolai's phone buzzed. He glanced at the screen. "Excuse me for a minute, Vanya. It's Pyotr Alekseevich."

"I got to go check some things in the garage. Come over when you're done here," Vanya said and stepped outside.

Nikolai nodded his agreement and answered Pyotr Alekseevich's call.

"I hope this does not complicate the situation more," Pyotr Alekseevich said. "Svetlana is coming back here next week, and she wants to bring our son to meet me. It's strange timing. She knows about the stress and the pressure of the Board meeting, but once she sets her mind to something, there's no stopping her."

"It's all right, but I appreciate that you told me."

As soon as their conversation was over, Nikolai had an idea. He kept thinking about it, and he was also trying to imagine how hard it would be to know you have a child and not see him for so many years. It was a difficult situation for Pyotr Alekseevich and that added to Nikolai's doubts about the plan that was shaping itself in his mind. He cast all the doubts aside. *Na voine kak na voine*, a war is a war, and all methods are fair.

Nikolai dialed Anatoly's number and told him about the arrival of Pyotr Alekseevich's son and ex-wife.

"Anatoly, I have an idea about that. Hear me out." Nikolai started talking, and Anatoly listened quietly and attentively.

After Nikolai finished his explanation, he paused waiting for Anatoly's reaction.

"Not a bad idea, but a little questionable ethically," Anatoly said. "Not sure what the law would say about it."

"I only have one law, and that is to save the life of my client," Nikolai said.

"Under the circumstances, I agree," Anatoly said. "Let's do it."

Nikolai left the relative warmth of the security office and went inside the much colder garage. Vanya was just finishing cleaning Pyotr Alekseevich's BMW. He picked up the makeshift mirror device that Nikolai had made, and started looking under the carriage.

"You taught me well," he said to Nikolai. "A new step in my car-cleaning routine."

"And the most important one. You may have to do it first thing in the morning again."

"Why is that?"

"Svetlana and Pyotr Alekseevich's son are coming tomorrow, and they'll need to be picked up at the airport."

"She can't wait, I see? Moved up her arrival by a day? I always thought those two would get back together, but what weird timing."

"It's okay. We can handle it," Nikolai said. "Just send the car."

The next morning, as planned, Nikolai called Vanya to check on the arrival of Svetlana and her son.

"They're here. Everything is fine," Vanya said. "What about the computer virus? Have you heard from Viktor?"

"Yes. Oleg was telling the truth. The virus is innocuous. It didn't do anything bad to our system besides slowing it down."

"That's good to know," Vanya said. "Still, what a trickster that Oleg is."

"And do you know what JS stands for?" Nikolai said.

"How would I know? I don't understand computers at all."

"Job Security. And that's exactly what Oleg was after."

"Clever. Very clever," Vanya said. "And how do we know he's not going to do this kind of stuff again?"

"I think he's learned his lesson," Nikolai said. "And we have bigger problems to solve now anyway. Where is Pyotr Alekseevich's family?"

"I sent them to the conference room. Pyotr Alekseevich will be there as soon as he's free. You guys really take good care of your clients and their families," Vanya said.

"How so?" Nikolai said.

"Svetlana said that Anatoly took them to the airport himself. Quite a boss you have."

"I'm not surprised. Thanks, Vanya," Nikolai said. "I'll go greet them."

Svetlana, dressed in jeans, boots, and a warm sweater, sat on a couch in the conference room. A cup of steaming tea was in front of her on the low table. In the corner, two secretaries were busy making copies and putting them in folders, probably in preparation for the Board meeting.

"Nice to see you again, Nikolai," Svetlana said.

Nikolai came up and shook her extended hand. "The pleasure is mine."

Their greetings were interrupted by grunting sounds.

"The wheel is broken, the wheel is broken," a deep male voice said. "Mommy, look! The wheel is broken."

A young man who looked like he was about nineteen or twenty years old crawled out from behind the couch, a small toy car in his large masculine hands. He was dressed in dark pants, a loose-fitting bright blue sweatshirt, and scuffed-up sneakers. His face was contorted with pain and disgust. "The wheel is broken," he kept repeating, pointing to the car in his hands.

"It's okay, we'll fix it. Don't worry," Svetlana said. "Let mommy take a look."

She picked up the car and looked at it. The young man crawled back to the other side of the couch. "I need to find a new toy in my bag," he said. "A toy that works."

Svetlana glanced at the secretaries, then turned to Nikolai. "That's how it has been all these years. He turned four, and that was it. Never got past that age, it seems like." She sighed.

The door opened and Pyotr Alekseevich walked in. "Svetlana, nice to see you."

The young man crawled out from behind the couch again. This time, he was clutching a small teddy bear in his hands. He plopped on a chair next to Svetlana and stared at Pyotr Alekseevich. "Mommy, who's that?" he said.

"Ilia, it's your daddy," Svetlana said to the young man.

Ilia inched closer to Svetlana, his eyes darting from Pyotr Alekseevich to Svetlana before stopping on Pyotr Alekseevich's face. "Can you fix this car?" Ilia asked and handed him the broken toy.

Nikolai saw the expression of shock on Pyotr Alekseevich's face that was quickly replaced by a wide forced smile. "I'm sure we can figure something out." He took the car from Ilia.

Not wanting to add to this already uncomfortable situation, Nikolai quietly walked out of the room.

Later that night, Viktor called Nikolai again.

"I have some new information. Pretty interesting stuff," Viktor said.

"I'm listening."

"You know that I'm a thorough guy, right? But my methods are not always exactly by the book, and you know that, too. So, while I was checking your network, I looked into Luna Oil, and found that they had the same virus, JS-67."

"Looked into it?" Nikolai said.

"All right. Hacked into it, but it's just semantics. I wanted to make sure the two companies got equal treatment from your local computer guy. And they did. But I also found something weird. I don't know if it means anything, but I thought I'd tell you."

"What is it?"

"Somebody in Luna Oil has been doing a lot of research on that big oil spill that happened in Alaska a few years ago."

"You mean Exxon Valdez?" Nikolai said.

"That's the one. Whoever was doing it got into all kinds of little details about it, from water quality to the way the oil spread and traveled, to all kinds of graphs and charts about contaminants and what not."

"Luna Oil is an oil company, so somebody might be interested in other oil companies, what's so strange about it?"

"That's what I thought at first, too."

"And then what?"

"I kept looking at their browsing history, and what seemed odd that there were no traces of any other research, about anything, just that oil spill."

"Do you think Luna Oil is somehow involved with Exxon?" Nikolai said.

"I wondered about that. What do you think? Could it be?"

"Highly unlikely."

"I agree. It's something else, but I can't figure out what it can be."

"I think I have an idea," Nikolai said and turned on his laptop. There was research he needed to do.

Chapter Twelve

In the office next morning, Nikolai asked Pyotr Alekseevich to see the latest environmental reports. When Pyotr Alekseevich heard Nikolai's request, his expression registered surprise with a hint of annoyance.

"Nikolai, I appreciate your interest, but what can you do with the environmental reports? The numbers show high contamination, with all the graphs and charts to support it." Pyotr Alekseevich shook his head. "You're a great bodyguard and an excellent security expert, but you're not a petroleum engineer and not a chemist."

"Just let me see them, and I'll tell you more."

"Fine." Pyotr Alekseevich handed him the folder. "Just don't ask me to explain anything. I understand about a third of this report. I'm not a chemist either."

Nikolai opened the folder and compared the numbers and the graphs to the information he downloaded from the Exxon Valdez oil spill report. And he saw exactly what he had expected to see after talking to Viktor.

"Pyotr Alekseevich, you have to look at this."

With obvious reluctance, Pyotr Alekseevich got up and walked over to the desk where Nikolai spread out all the information.

"Exxon Valdez? What does that have to do with us? That spill happened a few years ago in Alaska," Pyotr Alekseevich said.

"Take a closer look," Nikolai said.

Pyotr Alekseevich leaned over the table and started looking at the charts and graphs.

"This is our data. And this one is from Exxon's spill," Nikolai said. "Compare them."

Pyotr Alekseevich studied both documents carefully for a few minutes, then looked up at Nikolai. "They are identical. Very odd. How could this be? You aren't telling me that their oil got into our river? That's impossible."

"No, that's not it," Nikolai said, letting Pyotr Alekseevich process this information.

"So, it's some mistake?" Pyotr Alekseevich said.

"It's no mistake. I don't think MENDAX did any testing. They got the numbers and graphs from the Exxon Valdez report and sent them to you," Nikolai said.

Pyotr Alekseevich looked straight at Nikolai. "But why would they do such a thing?"

"Do you know who owns MENDAX?" Nikolai said.

"No, but it sounds like you do, and it means something. Just tell me."

"MENDAX is owned by a large conglomerate company, and Denis Fedorovich Petrenko is on the Board of that company."

"Denis is? The brother-in-law of the old director?" Pyotr Alekseevich's expression registered amazement and disbelief. "I knew that they owned Luna Oil, but I thought that their other business was toy stores and other retail stuff."

"They have that, too. But they also own MENDAX."

"Let me see those results again," Pyotr Alekseevich said and pulled the graphs closer. For a few moments, he inspected the graphs quietly, then he pushed them aside and looked at Nikolai. "Are you thinking what I'm thinking?"

Nikolai nodded. "I'm pretty sure. MENDAX wanted to make it look like there was a major leak so that the company got in more trouble with the government, on top of the unpaid taxes. So, they copied the Exxon data, changed the labels, and sent it to you just before the Board meeting."

"And a copy to the government, of course, providing another reason to sell the company," Pyotr Alekseevich added. "Nikolai, I'm impressed. How did you figure it out?"

140

"I had some help," Nikolai said. "Viktor, the computer guy who works for Centurion, poked around and found some of these graphs on Luna Oil computers. Somebody there is very interested in bringing your company down. And now we know who."

Pyotr Alekseevich nodded. "I expected a lot of things from Denis, but I certainly did not expect this. I didn't think he would go that far to destroy my company."

"What are you going to do now?" Nikolai said.

"Order an independent environmental evaluation," Pyotr Alekseevich said and reached for his phone.

Nikolai left Pyotr Alekseevich to deal with the environmental evaluation and focused on the next, and the main, challenge. And that was the Board meeting itself.

Nikolai and Vanya had practiced the routine enough to perform it with the utmost precision, and they predicted, calculated, and worked out their actions in all possible circumstances: a trip to the airport in an armored car, a special permission to drive the car onto the airfield, a quick and uneventful transition of the two Board members from the airplane to the car, and a safe journey back to the compound.

From his training, Nikolai knew that entering and exiting cars and buildings, and other transitional movements were the most dangerous for the clients and their bodyguards. So, when the car left the airport and turned onto the main road leading to Upper Luzinsk, the two Board members and their luggage safely inside, Nikolai breathed a sigh of relief. Next stop was the compound, and the situation there would be much easier to control.

Vanya was driving, so Nikolai leaned back in the front passenger seat next to him and watched the bleak landscape roll by: the tall mounds of snow, the dwarf trees, and the low darkening sky. Vanya tuned the radio to a classical music station and turned the volume to low.

Even after staying in Upper Luzinsk for the last few weeks, Nikolai could not get used to this strange place, so isolated, so cold, and so different from the big city that he was used to. He peeked into the visor mirror at their distinguished passengers, curious about their reaction to Upper Luzinsk. Neither of them seemed to be paying attention to the outside world. The woman, a slim redhead in fashionable glasses and wearing lots of fur, was busy with her phone.

She reminded him of Olga: good-looking, elegant, and always busy.

Nikolai glanced at the man. In contrast to the woman, he was dressed quite plainly, in jeans and a thick parka. He, too, was busy. But not with the phone. The man was leafing through a thick stack of papers he put on his lap on top of his briefcase. One of those papers was probably that document to be signed in the next few days, the document that was causing all this hectic activity and Nikolai's agency's protection.

They had just passed a small intersection with a narrow road leading to a fishing village when Nikolai noticed a pair of lonely headlights shining into their car from behind. The headlights were approaching quickly.

"Someone's in a hurry," muttered Vanya and slowed down allowing the vehicle to pass, but it showed no such intention.

"Speed up then," Nikolai said. "We don't want them trailing us."

The vehicle was behaving strangely, mirroring Vanya's actions: when Vanya slowed down, so did the car behind them, and when Vanya accelerated, the other car did, too. The bright headlights made it difficult to discern what kind of car it was, but from its boxy silhouette and relatively small size, Nikolai was pretty sure it was a Soviet-made Lada, a run-of-the-mill inexpensive vehicle.

"Should we be worried about this?" Vanya said.

"I don't know yet," Nikolai said and checked his gun. "Lock the doors," he quietly said to Vanya.

Their two passengers seemed oblivious to the unfolding events, and Nikolai decided not to say anything to them. No need to worry them. At least not yet.

Vanya slowed down once more, and the old Lada started passing on the left.

Hugging the snowy curb, Vanya slowed down, too.

"Just an erratic driver, probably," Vanya said as the Lada got ahead of them.

The Lada accelerated, moved into the center of the lane in front of them and rapidly slowed down, coming to a full stop in front of them. Vanya slammed on the brakes, forcing everyone in the car to lurch forward. Nikolai heard a loud thump, the screeching of metal hitting metal, and the screaming of their two passengers, all of it seemed to be happening at once. Their car skidded to a stop, and Nikolai turned to check on the passengers: they were frightened but not hurt.

"What is going on?" the redhead said. "Are you not paying attention to the road? Do something!"

"I will when I need to," Nikolai said, trying to calculate what could happen next. The damage to both cars was obvious: Lada's rear was mangled, and so was the front of their car.

Two men came out of the Lada. They were both young, probably in their mid-twenties, and both dressed in bulky coats that could, and probably did, conceal weapons. One was tall and athletic-looking, with broad shoulders and muscular legs. The other was shorter, with most of his strength located in his upper body, with smaller legs. Guys who favored push-ups over squats tended to look like that.

The two men approached their car.

"What do they want?" the redhead said.

"Money," her colleague said. "They pulled in front of us on purpose."

"How do you know? You weren't even looking," the redhead said. "And what money do they want? Why?"

"Standard maneuver of thugs and extortionists," the man said. "And the car is old, so it figures they want money."

"What do you think?" the redhead asked Nikolai.

"I agree," Nikolai said and turned to Vanya. "It's best if we give them money. To pay for the damage."

"Are you crazy?" Vanya said. "I'm not giving them any money. That's the only reason they did what they did. I'll show them!"

Vanya stepped out of the car, slammed the door shut behind him, and started arguing with the two guys. Nikolai could not make out the words but the tension and anger were obvious. Still in his seat, Nikolai slipped his gun out of its holster and cocked it.

"Do something!" the redhead said again.

"They could kill Vanya!" the man said. "Help him!"

"My job is to protect the two of you," Nikolai responded. "And right now, there is no immediate danger to either of you. And not even to Vanya."

"What?" the redhead said. "That's callous! He needs help! They'll kill him!"

The taller of the two men came up to the car on the driver's side and pulled on the handle. The shorter one was still arguing with Vanya.

Nikolai got out of the car from the passenger's side and took a small step towards the front of the car so that the young man's hands were in Nikolai's sight. "Step away from the car!" Nikolai said loudly, keeping his eyes on the man's hands: his left hand was still on the door handle, and he used his right hand to support himself on the body of the car. There were no weapons in the young man's hands. In contrast to Nikolai, the young man kept his gaze straight on Nikolai's face, not even trying to see what Nikolai's hands were doing. That indicated to Nikolai that the man was an amateur. You couldn't kill with your face.

"Step away from the car," Nikolai repeated.

"And what if I don't?" the young man said, his tone menacing.

Nikolai raised his hand, with his Makarov pistol in it, straight up in the air and fired a shot.

"Don't shoot! Don't shoot!" the young man screamed, his expression quickly going from confident to panicked. "Are you crazy?" He backed away from the car.

The shorter man was no longer focused on Vanya. He was watching Nikolai from a distance.

"Hands in the air! Both of you!" Nikolai said, pointing the gun to the shorter man and motioning for the two of them to come closer to each other. "Now! Or the next shot will be at you."

Fear obvious on their faces, both young men raised their hands in the air.

"Face down on the ground!" Nikolai ordered. "Count to one hundred. Loudly and slowly. And don't get up until you're done."

The two men dropped to the ground.

"He's a psycho," muttered the shorter one and started counting.

"Vanya, get their key," Nikolai said, still pointing the gun to the two men now lying face down on the snow.
Vanya reached into the Lada, took the key out of the ignition and threw it far into a snowdrift.

"Now get in the car," Nikolai said.

Vanya opened the driver's door and got in. Nikolai sat down next to him.

"Let's go," Nikolai said.

Vanya started the ignition, and they sped off towards the compound, leaving the mangled Lada and the two men behind.

"What was that all about?" the redhead asked.

"Money," Nikolai said. "It's racket. They take an old car, create an accident with a nicer car, and demand money for repairs. Much more than needed. Then, they repair the car themselves and use the money as they wish."

"What do the police here do about it?" the man asked Vanya.

"The police? Best case scenario, they do nothing. Or else, they are part of the scam."

"That's what I thought. Things are the same everywhere," the man said.

The next two days went by quietly and uneventfully, exactly the way Nikolai had planned. Finally, Nikolai felt that all the work that he and Vanya had put in was paying off. Of course, their job was far from over as they were constantly monitoring everyone's movements.

In the day time, they focused their efforts on Pyotr Alekseevich's building and the conference room, and at night they put extra security in and around the hotel where the Board members and Pyotr Alekseevich were staying. After the incident on the road, it did not take a lot of convincing to get Pyotr Alekseevich to move from his apartment into the hotel for the duration of the Board meeting.

146

Meal times were the most challenging. As Nikolai knew well from his experiences and training, the clients were the most vulnerable when they were moving around. And the two Board members insisted on walking to the restaurant from the building despite Nikolai's and Vanya's warnings that it may be dangerous. The redhead was especially adamant about being able to walk.

"It's bad enough to be confined to this compound and have you two as constant company," she said to Vanya and Nikolai. "I don't want to have any more restrictions. I'm beginning to feel like I'm the criminal being guarded, not a client being protected. If something happens, so be it."

Vanya was about to argue, but Nikolai stopped him. "Arguing won't win us any favors. She's stubborn, and she will only make our job difficult if we try to fight her. It's a short walk, so let's just offer some extra protection."

It was not the best turn of events, but at least Upper Luzinsk was not a big city populated with many people and crowded with hard-to-control objects. Since most of the movement of the Board members was inside the compound, Nikolai was confident that the situation was under control. Still, confident did not mean sloppy or careless, so he made sure that everyone, including Nikolai himself, stayed vigilant.

Finally, it was after lunch on the last day of meetings. The final documents were supposed to be signed that afternoon. After that, the Board members were going back to Moscow, and so was Nikolai. Andrei was scheduled to stay as long as Natalya, and especially her dad, wanted him to stay.

Nikolai walked Pyotr Alekseevich to the conference room after lunch and returned to the security office. He was hungry and looked forward to eating lunch he brought from the restaurant for Vanya and himself. He had just put in the bowl with the chicken and mashed potatoes into the microwave when the door to the office opened.

Pyotr Alekseevich stuck his head inside. His parka was open, and Nikolai saw that the director was wearing a business suit, his white shirt starched to perfection, and his blue tie accentuating his triumphant smile. "I'll owe you guys some champagne later today. We're almost done. I'm going to my office right now to get one more paper that Natalya is translating, and that's it. We'll be signing right afterwards and having a celebration tonight. You two are definitely invited."

"I'm coming with you," Nikolai said.

"No need. Andrei is with me." Pyotr Alekseevich smiled again and closed the door.

The microwave dinged. Nikolai took out the bowl of steaming chicken and mashed potatoes and put it on the table, next to the plates and silverware.

"That's a relief." Vanya put some of the food on his plate and pushed the bowl towards Nikolai. "I guess all our activity scared off the bad guys. You're younger than me, Nikolai, but I have to tell you I learned a lot from you. And I even started to like you."

"Thanks, Vanya. Me, too." Nikolai took a bite of his food.

"So, are you heading back tomorrow?"

"Yes, on the morning charter flight, with everyone else. If you ever want to come visit, please do. You can stay with me. It looks like I'll have my apartment all to myself, so there's plenty of room. Have you ever been to Moscow?"

"Just once, years ago, and under pretty strange circumstances."

"How's that?" Nikolai said.

"My wife and I went one summer. We planned to do some sightseeing, you know, the Kremlin, the Red Square, the museums. She likes to read about the tsars and wanted to see all the historical places. So, we picked August one year, and when we arrived, we landed in the middle of all that chaos." Vanya shook his head. "Unbelievable. The one time we went to visit, and there was that coup. We didn't know if we were going to get out alive. So much for museums. I don't want to go there again."

Nikolai chuckled. "Come on, Vanya. That was a long time ago. We don't have coups and revolutions every summer. You can come again. Moscow is very different now. More glamorous, cleaner, and nicer. Lots of things to see."

"If I have you as a tour guide and a bodyguard, I just might." Vanya smiled.

"It would be my pleasure."

As Nikolai thought back to the coup, Natalya's words came to his mind.

I was little but I remember how happy my parents were when the soldiers and all the tanks sent to the Parliament disobeyed their military orders...

My mom always told me that it was the deciding factor in the outcome of the coup...

We were all cheering and eating ice-cream...

But Natalya's mom died when Natalya was too young to discuss politics.

"Vanya, what year was the coup? It was 1991, wasn't it?" Nikolai put down his fork as a sudden thought produced a wave of cold sweat.

"It sure was," Vanya said without looking up, his attention still on his lunch.

"That's more than twenty years ago."

"Unbelievable," Vanya said. "Time goes by so quickly."

"Vanya, there is no way Natalya could remember anything about that coup. She was much too young, so she couldn't have been there. She wasn't there." Nikolai was standing now, checking his holster.

Vanya looked at him with confusion. "What has that got to do with Natalya?"

"She's our murderer. Alert all posts. I'm going to Pyotr's office." Nikolai jumped up and rushed out of the security office.

Chapter Thirteen

As fast as he could, Nikolai raced to Pyotr Alekseevich's office hoping to catch him on the way. From the corner of the hallway, Nikolai could see that the door to the office was closed, and Andrei was sitting on the chair right outside Pyotr's office, facing the door. He looked like he was dozing off.

"Andrei!" Nikolai called out. "Wake up! Now!" He ran up to Andrei, took one look at him and gasped. Andrei's open jacket revealed the front of his shirt, all soaked in blood. His eyes, wide-open, were clearly lifeless. A small puddle of blood formed on the floor under his chair. Nikolai reached for Andrei's holster under his jacket. Andrei's Makarov pistol was gone.

On the floor next to Andrei was an empty tea cup. It smelled minty and earthy.

Natalya's secret recipe.

Nikolai pushed and pulled at the doorknob, but the door would not budge.

"Pyotr Alekseevich, are you there? Can you hear me?"

No answer.

Nikolai dialed Vanya's number.

"Vanya, what do you see on the monitors? Where's Natalya?" Nikolai was now half-way up the steps to the second floor where the conference room was located.

"Nothing so far. It's all quiet, and no sign of Natalya."

"She killed Andrei, took his gun and is probably headed to the conference room."

Vanya gasped. "Andrei is dead?"

"Where's Pyotr Alekseevich? Is he in the conference room?" Nikolai said. "We need to check and secure the room."

"I'm coming," Vanya said. "Wait, Nikolai, I see somebody. A man in a ski-mask is walking towards Pyotr Alekseevich's office. Be careful!"

As soon as Vanya said it, Nikolai heard a gunshot, then another through the receiver. "Vanya, are you okay?"

"I'm fine, but somebody just shot two cameras. I'll call you when I get to the conference room."

"All right. I'm going to check Pyotr Alekseevich's office."

Bracing himself to face the unknown horror that probably waited for him inside, Nikolai rushed back to Pyotr Alekseevich's office, drew his gun, and said loudly, "It's Nikolai, and I'm armed. Who's in there? Can you hear me?"

After a brief pause, he heard Natalya's voice, "You'd better hear me, Mr. Bodyguard. I'm armed, too, and I have Pyotr."

"Let me talk to him. Pyotr Alekseevich, can you hear me?"

"Yes, Nikolai, I can hear you." There was a mix of anger and resignation in Pyotr Alekseevich's voice.

"Please try to stay calm and do what Natalya tells you to do. We will get you out of this. You promised me champagne tonight, and I'm determined to keep you to that promise."

"That's enough." Natalya's voice interrupted their conversation. She sounded agitated. That was a bad sign. Agitated people tended to lose control, and armed agitated people who had lost control could cause some serious damage.

Nikolai drew in a deep breath and started talking in a calm voice. "Natalya, let him go. You're getting yourself in more trouble than you can imagine."

"I'm in a lot of trouble already, so I don't care what happens now."

"That's not true. You let him go, and we'll forget all about it."

"I have nothing to lose."

"Your freedom," Nikolai said.

"I've lost it after I shot Andrei."

"You let Pyotr Alekseevich go, and I'll let you go. You'll have time to leave the country. Remember Cyprus?"

"I'm listening," Natalya said.

"I'm not the police, and my only interest is in protecting my client. Just let him go."

"Only if you fulfill my demands."

Nikolai felt his tension release just a little. At least she was willing to negotiate.

"What are your demands?" he said.

"Are you taking notes? First, I want the sales contract from the Board room. That's for starters."

"Let me work on this."

"And that's not all."

Nikolai heard loud approaching footsteps. He turned around to see Vanya running up to the office, his expression panicked.

"I have more bad news for you," Vanya said. "Mikhail took Svetlana and the receptionist girl hostage, and Svetlana's son is going crazy outside the door. They are in the break room downstairs."

"Mikhail? The one who killed that guard?"

"Yes, him. He must have been that man in the mask I saw on the monitors."

"Natalya, did you hear this?" Nikolai said. "Mikhail has Svetlana and the receptionist."

"I know. We planned it together," Natalya said calmly. "The next thing we need is a car for Mikhail. After we have the sales contract."

"I need a little bit of time," Nikolai said. "Let me and Vanya go talk to him."

"Make it quick."

"Natalya, I think you're making a mistake. It's not too late to stop. I'm not a cop, so I will let you go. Just let Pyotr Alekseevich go. I don't care about anything else. I just want him safe."

"Go talk to Mikhail. Now!" She raised her voice.

Nikolai and Vanya hurried to the break room. Outside of it, two armed guards were trying to subdue Ilia, but he was fighting them off, yelling and screaming, "I want my mommy! Mommy! Mommy!"

"Mikhail, can you hear me?" Nikolai said through the door. "I just talked to Natalya. We understand your demands and we will get a car for you, but please let Svetlana go. Her son is going crazy here, and you won't be able to handle two hostages at the same time. Please let Svetlana go."

Ilia's screaming was getting louder and more violent. He started throwing himself against the door.

"We can't control this kid," Nikolai said. "Have mercy, Mikhail. He needs his mother. He's sick, and he and Svetlana have nothing to do with any of this. They will just be a burden to you."

"Mommy! Mommy!" Ilia kept yelling and banging on the door with his fists.

"All right, but step away from the door. Everyone, or I'll shoot!"

"Mikhail, we've all stepped away, but I can't do anything with Ilia. He needs Svetlana."

"Here!" The door opened and Mikhail pushed out Svetlana, her eyes wide open with fear and her dark hair disheveled. At that same moment, Ilia threw open the door, pushed Svetlana out of the way and pointed a gun at Mikhail's head. "Hands in the air! One wrong move or one wrong word, and I'll shoot you."

Chapter Fourteen

Mikhail lifted his hands up as his face registered shock and disbelief. "But I thought you were..."

"I spent a year acting." Ilia shoved Mikhail face down to the floor. "Be quiet, or I'll shoot you." Ilia took a pair of handcuffs out of his jacket pocket, and snapped them on Mikhail's hands. "And you'd better do what we tell you. No surprises and no sudden moves. Get up!"

Svetlana rushed back into the room and came back out with the young receptionist who was physically unharmed but sobbing uncontrollably. Svetlana took her aside, and they both sat down on the floor, comforting each other.

Mikhail, his hands clasped behind his back, struggled to his feet.

"Get ready to talk to Natalya," Nikolai said to Mikhail. "And don't even think of doing anything stupid. I'll shoot you on the spot."

Nikolai dialed Natalya's number. "I'm here with Mikhail, and we just got the car. It's right outside the entrance."

"Let me hear Mikhail," Natalya said.

Nikolai held the phone next to Mikhail's mouth. "Tell Natalya we're on our way to the car."

"We're on the way," Mikhail said.

"Are you inside the car? Start it then and let me hear the engine."

"Not yet," Nikolai responded.

"Get Mikhail in the car and let him call me next time. And make sure you and Vanya are not there," Natalya said. "And you two come back here. Now!"

Nikolai clicked off and had two of the guards escort Mikhail to the front entrance where a car was waiting.

"Let's go back to Pyotr Alekseevich's office," Nikolai said to Vanya.

"So Ilia is not sick?" Vanya said. "What was that all about?"

"He's not sick, and he's not their son. He works for our agency."

Minutes later, they were at Pyotr Alekseevich's office. Nikolai leaned towards the door and listened. Three other guards positioned himself at stairwell exits.

"Are you in the car, Mikhail?" he heard Natalya's voice. "Good. Now ask to switch cars. I don't trust anyone here. And call me back."

"Natalya, Vanya and I are back," Nikolai said. "As you asked. Right, Vanya?"

"We're here," Vanya said.

"Do you have the sales contract for me?" Natalya said.

"Not yet, but I can send Vanya for it. Should he take it straight to the car?"

"NO! Bring it to me. I want to make sure you're not playing with me."

"I don't know where it is or what it looks like. Please ask Pyotr Alekseevich," Vanya said.

"Vanya," Pyotr Alekseevich said. "The contract is in the blue folder, with all the other documents. It's on the conference room table. Please bring the whole folder."

"Will do!" Vanya said. Nikolai motioned for him to leave.

Through the door, he heard Natalya's phone ring. "Yes, Mikhail? Got a different car? Good. We'll be there soon, as soon as we get the sales contract."

A few minutes later, Vanya came running, huffing and winded from the trip. In his hands, he had a blue folder. "Got it!"

"Natalya, we have the contract," Nikolai said.

"Slide it under the door and get out of the building. All of you."

"But what about Pyotr Alekseevich?"

"What about him?"

"You need to release him when you get in the car," Nikolai said.

"That would be too easy, wouldn't it? I'll release him once we're out of the front gate. He can walk back. And don't even think of following us."

"All right. I'm leaving now. You're free to go."

Nikolai motioned for Vanya and other guards to leave the building. "Wait at the front gate," he said loudly. "On the outside. And as soon as Pyotr Alekseevich is out of the car, let me know." Then, he whispered to Vanya, "Call the police and the ambulance."

Nikolai left the hallway, walked away from the main staircase and down the narrow fire escape staircase, equipped with fire extinguishers and fire alarm buttons, to the first floor. He hoped that his calculation was correct. Pyotr Alekseevich's life and the fate of the company depended on it.

When he reached the first floor, Nikolai crouched in the dark corner under the staircase, took a deep breath, steadying his nerves, and waited. For a while, everything was quiet. No footsteps, no doors opening or closing, just dead silence. A few minutes ago, Nikolai was ready to bet his life on this move, and now a tiny shadow of doubt crept in. What if he was wrong? He chased away the thought and focused on keeping still in his hiding spot. It was getting more difficult as his leg was starting to hurt from lack of movement. He slowly rubbed it, relieving the ache, and kept waiting.

After a few more long quiet moments, he heard a door slam up above him, followed by two sets of footsteps, going down, lower and lower. Nikolai peeked out of the corner and saw two figures going down. The light was dim, but he could clearly see that it was Pyotr Alekseevich and Natalya. Pyotr Alekseevich was in the front, Natalya right behind him, a pistol pointed to his head. Andrei's pistol, no doubt.

Nikolai let them take a few more steps down as he kept crouching in the corner.

When Natalya was right next to Nikolai, he jumped up, grabbed and twisted her arm with the pistol, sending the pistol flying into the corner. Pyotr Alekseevich rushed to get the gun, but Natalya was quicker.

She dove to the ground and rolled, loosening Nikolai's grip on her arm. As he tried to take a hold of her again, she kicked him, hurting his bad leg and freeing herself completely. Immediately, she leapt after the pistol. It ricocheted off the wall of the narrow hallway, and Natalya grabbed it. She pointed the pistol at Nikolai and back-kicked Pyotr Alekseevich, sending him to the ground.

Natalya took a step sideways so that both Nikolai and Pyotr Alekseevich were in her field of vision. Now, her pistol was pointed at both of them. Nikolai's pistol was pointed at her. Nikolai shifted to the side.

"What are you doing?" Natalya said. "Stand still!"

"It's just my old wound aching," Nikolai said and bent his knee.

"You're not so invincible after all, are you?" Natalya said.

"I guess not," Nikolai said quietly. Grimacing in pain, he leaned against the wall. He knew exactly what he needed to do, and he hoped he remembered a small but important detail about the wall behind him. He put his back flat against the wall, pushing the fire alarm button. The sudden and loud wailing of the alarm startled Natalya for just a moment, but a moment was all Nikolai needed. He drew his gun and shot Natalya in the arm. As the bullet grazed her flesh, she dropped the pistol. This time, it was Pyotr Alekseevich who grabbed it.

Nikolai dropped Natalya on the ground, took a pair of plastic handcuffs out of his pocket and handcuffed her. Then, he wrapped his scarf around her wounded arm to stop the bleeding.

"Still saving me?" Natalya said. "What, it makes you feel good about yourself?"

"It's in my contract," Nikolai said.

In the distance, he heard the wailing of police sirens.

Vanya burst through the door, his gun drawn.

"We're okay, Vanya. Put the gun down," Nikolai said.

"Pyotr Alekseevich, you aren't wounded, are you?" Vanya asked. "And you, Nikolai?"

"No, we're fine," Pyotr Alekseevich said.

Nikolai glanced at Pyotr Alekseevich's ashen face. "It's over now," Nikolai said. "You'll be fine."

Pyotr Alekseevich nodded. "Thank you, Nikolai."

When two uniformed police officers walked in to take Natalya away, Nikolai picked up the blue folder that Natalya dropped in the struggle and handed it to Pyotr Alekseevich. "It's all yours now. And so is the company."

As Nikolai, Vanya, and Pyotr Alekseevich stepped outside, Vanya excused himself and left to check on the others.

Svetlana came running up to them. "Pyotr!" She hugged him. "I'm so glad you're all right."

"Me, too." He hugged her, too, then pulled back, as if suddenly realizing something. "Where's Ilia? Is he okay?"

"There's something you need to know," Svetlana said. "I am really sorry..."

"Is he wounded?" Pyotr Alekseevich said, his expression turning somber. "Has something happened to him?"

"No, no, he is not wounded," Svetlana said. "It's not that."

"Let me explain," Nikolai said, "since all this was my idea." He turned to Pyotr Alekseevich. "I'm going to spare you the extra worries and just say it the way it is. Ilia is not your son. Your son is not here. And neither of them has any developmental challenges or disabilities."

"What? I don't understand." Pyotr Alekseevich looked at Svetlana, then at Nikolai.

"It was all an act, to help protect you. Ilia works for our agency, and when Svetlana said she was coming here with your son, that seemed like a perfect opportunity to bring him in, undercover." Nikolai lightly touched Pyotr Alekseevich's arm. "And it was all my idea. Svetlana only agreed to it because I convinced her that Ilia's presence could help save your life."

"And it looks like your plan worked, Nikolai. Thank you," Pyotr Alekseevich said. "Is Ilia his real name, by the way?"

"Yes, it is, just like your son's. And that's a coincidence," Nikolai said.

Pyotr Alekseevich paused for a moment, as if absorbing all this information. Then, he addressed Svetlana. "Where's our real son?"

"Still in Moscow. I told him all about you, and he really wants to meet you. He was disappointed when I had to change our plans at the last minute, but he understands that a Board meeting can be stressful and agreed to wait until after it's over. Plus, his engineering professor assigned a big project at the last minute, so staying in Moscow and working on it was the best choice for him."

"He is studying engineering?" Pyotr Alekseevich sounded surprised.

"And he's a pretty good student," Svetlana said.

Pyotr Alekseevich smiled and hugged her again. Nikolai watched the two of them step away from the building, the blinding spotlights and blinking police lights. They kept hugging and talking quietly. They looked relieved and happy.

Then, he heard a car door open and close as the police put Natalya in the back of their van.

Vanya came up to Nikolai. "I did not suspect her at all," Vanya said.

"Me neither," Nikolai said. "But I should have thought about it more. The whole bodyguard assignment seemed strange from the beginning. I totally missed it."

"Why would she do something like this?" Vanya said.

"I don't know her whole story, but I know that it's because of money," Nikolai said. "It's always because of money. And she wanted to go to Cyprus, remember? I don't think Cyprus has an extradition treaty with Russia, so she was really playing us when she talked about it, sunny beaches and all."

"Just like when she talked about the 1991 coup, right?" Vanya said.

"Yes. And I should have caught on, but I didn't. I got too used to her, and I trusted her too much. Criminals always make mistakes or get too bold, and that's how they get caught," Nikolai said. "I made a big mistake with Natalya, a mistake that cost Andrei his life."

"How did you know to go to the fire escape, not to the main exit?"

"Two things. One, Natalya was too quick to agree to release Pyotr Alekseevich outside the front gate. It felt too easy, like she was planning something else. And two, she

162

insisted on having the contract with her, not in the car. That made me think that she would not even be in that car, and that all this fuss with Mikhail and changing cars was a distraction. She wanted all the attention at the front while she would go to the back and into that tunnel."

"What was she planning to do about Mikhail?" Vanya said.

"Nothing, most likely," Nikolai said. "As far as she was concerned, Mikhail's only purpose was to distract our attention. Of course, he thought he was a real partner with Natalya. She tricked him, too. And now he's going to be serving time for the murder of that guard and for kidnapping."

A young man, one of Nikolai's team, came up to them and addressed Nikolai. "As you asked, we checked that area behind the compound and found a Jeep there.

Don't know why it's there or who it belongs to, but you were right. It's there, and the keys were in it." He handed the keys to Nikolai.

Vanya looked at Nikolai with admiration. "That was supposed to be Natalya's getaway car, right?"

Nikolai nodded. "It looks like it."

"You're good," Vanya said. "Really good."

"Not good enough," Nikolai said. "I lost Andrei."

Chapter Fifteen

In Moscow, the trees were still devoid of spring leaves and the air was still cold, but the bright blue sky was already illuminated by the first warm rays of the spring sun. For the first time since the dramatic events in Upper Luzinsk, Nikolai felt a sense of peace when he and Vanya entered Vagankovo Cemetery through the massive gates and walked past the small vendor stands where elderly women in dark coats and colorful head scarves were selling flowers, small icons, and plastic vases.

At the entrance to the cemetery's main alley, Nikolai spotted Anatoly waiting for them, a large bouquet of white lilies in his hands. They greeted each other and walked past stone monuments, marble crosses, sculptures of angels, and large portraits in stone. A stream of water from the melting snow was running down the alley, sparkling and shining in the sun.

For a few moments they walked in silence, getting deeper and deeper into the sprawling alleys. It was a weekday, and the cemetery was mostly deserted except for a few workers tending to graves and picking up the old leaves that the melted snow revealed.

"This place is enormous," Vanya said.

"It's one of the oldest cemeteries in Moscow. Dates back to 18th century," Nikolai said. "Andrei liked coming here. He always said this place helped him calm down and think about what's really important."

They reached the end of the main alley and turned into a narrow lane. Anatoly opened a small gate and led them to Andrei's gravesite next to a new seedling.

"Good idea about planting this tree," Anatoly said.

"Andrei liked trees," Nikolai said, "especially the tall ones that create shade. And shadows. And this one will grow tall and strong."

Anatoly put the lilies next to a framed portrait of smiling Andrei on top of the fresh grave.

"We should start a collection for a monument," Nikolai said. "Andrei would have wanted it. What do you think, Anatoly?"

"We don't need to. It's all taken care of."

"By whom?" Nikolai said.

"Pyotr Alekseevich paid for it," Vanya said. "He felt that he owed it to Andrei."

They stood for a few more minutes, then slowly left Andrei's grave, closed the small gate behind them, and headed back to the exit.

"How could I have missed the obvious? All that time, Natalya was so close to me, and I never suspected her," Nikolai said.

"I still don't understand why she needed a bodyguard if she herself was a hired assassin," Vanya said.

"We were puzzling over the bodyguard question all that time, but in the wrong way. We did not see the real reason. She needed to have firearms, and she knew that she could not have brought them in herself. So, she hired someone to bring the firearms in for her. A bodyguard," Nikolai said. "And the dead guy was supposed to be me."

"What a plan," Vanya said.

"One thing I don't understand is the involvement of Natalya's father." Nikolai turned to Anatoly. "I thought he was a clean businessman."

"And that was a mistake on my part." Anatoly said. "I did not check his personal life thoroughly enough. He is clean, as far as his business is concerned. And so is his daughter."

"I don't follow you," Vanya said.

"The girl who called herself Natalya is not his real daughter. His real daughter, the real Natalya Abramova, lives in London. She's a student there."

"What's the connection between Natalya the assassin and him?" Nikolai said.

"The man who said he was her father has a gambling problem, and he ended up owing a large sum to some shady people. A really large sum. And they made a deal with him that they would forgive the debt if he pretended to be Natalya's father. He had no choice but to agree. If his boss at the bank found out about his gambling debts, he would be fired immediately. And he would still owe these people money," Anatoly said.

"I take it that these people had something to do with the old director of the company? And with the attack on Vasily Petrovich?" Vanya said.

"That's exactly right. And they have been arrested," Anatoly said.

"And who is Natalya, really? Was anything she told us about herself true?" Nikolai said.

"We don't know much about her yet. But the investigation is just starting," Anatoly said.

They came back to the main square of the cemetery just inside the gates. Nikolai promised to take Vanya on a brief sightseeing tour of Moscow, and Anatoly was heading back to the office.

Nikolai and Vanya were about to part ways with Anatoly at the gate when Anatoly's phone rang. He glanced at the number and motioned for Nikolai and Vanya to wait while he talked.

"How's your leg feeling?" Anatoly asked Nikolai after he finished the phone call.

"Doctor says it will ache for a while, especially in cold weather, but other than that, it's as good as new."

"Good to hear," Anatoly said. "Take today off. But after you put Vanya on the plane tomorrow, come by the office. Vasily Petrovich is eager to have you back. And there have been some interesting new developments he wants to discuss with you."

"I'll be there in the morning," Nikolai said. He waved goodbye to Anatoly and followed Vanya out of the cemetery and into the sunlit Moscow street. It was a perfect day for sightseeing.

Also by Julia Gousseva

Anya's Story

Moscow Dreams

Twelve Months of a Soviet Childhood: Short Stories

Firebird: Adventure One

The Lollipop: Adventure Two

Snowdrops: Adventure Three

Grandma Witch: Adventure Four

Tall Tales for Short People

Made in the USA
Monee, IL
16 December 2021